Mary Gaitskill's *Bad Behavior*

"Mary Gaitskill [is] a vital and gifted new writer whose work has unusual importance at this time. This is a collection I urge you to read and to read right—from beginning to end. When you get to the glorious last story, denser with life than many novels, you will have to be cold-blooded indeed not to find yourself crying, as much for the joy of art as for the pity and sorrow at the secret heart of all living things."

—George Garrett, *The New York Times Book Review*

"Stubbornly original, with the sort of rhythm and fine moments that flatten you out when you don't expect it, these stories are a pleasure to read."

—Alice Munro

"Gaitskill writes with such authority, such radar-perfect detail, that she is able to make even the most extreme situations seem real. She takes us on a meticulously observed documentary tour of [her characters'] inner and outer lives, giving us fierce portraits of individuals rather than a gallery of eccentric types."

—Michiko Kakutani, *The New York Times*

"Intriguingly tart . . . urban true grit."

—*People*

"Riveting. Gaitskill has managed to lyrically reveal life's underside."

—*Newsday*

"Gaitskill's prose is taut, tense; sentences snap with quick twists of logic and rhythm. . . . *Bad Behavior* vibrates with constant analysis, self-doubt and delightfully morbid analogies."

—*Village Voice*

"Funny, touching, fiercely honest, with an intelligent eye and sensitive ear on every page."

—Leonard Michaels

ALSO BY MARY GAITSKILL

Don't Cry

Da Capo Best Music Writing 2006 (editor)

Veronica

Because They Wanted To

Two Girls, Fat and Thin

Bad Behavior

stories

Mary Gaitskill

SIMON & SCHUSTER PAPERBACKS

New York   London   Toronto   Sydney

SIMON & SCHUSTER
1230 Avenue of the Americas
New York, NY 10020

This Simon & Schuster trade paperback edition July 2009

SIMON & SCHUSTER and colophon are registered trademarks of Simon & Schuster, Inc.

For information about special discounts for bulk purchases, please contact Simon & Schuster Special Sales at 1-866-506-1949 or business@simonandschuster.com.

The Simon & Schuster Speakers Bureau can bring authors to your live event. For more information or to book an event contact the Simon & Schuster Speakers Bureau at 1-866-248-3049 or visit our website at www.simonspeakers.com.

Designed by Kyoko Watanabe

Manufactured in the United States of America

3 5 7 9 10 8 6 4

Library of Congress Cataloging-in-Publication Data
Gaitskill, Mary.
Bad behavior : stories / Mary Gaitskill.
p.   cm.
1. City and town life—New York (State)—New York—Fiction.
2. Lower East Side (New York, N.Y.)—Fiction. I. Title.
PS3557.A36B3 2009
813'.54—dc22   2009015579

ISBN 978-1-4391-4887-7

To my sisters,
Jane and Martha

All the conventions conspire
To make this fort assume
The furniture of home;
Lest we should see where we are,
Lost in a haunted wood,
Children afraid of the night
Who have never been happy or good.

—W. H. Auden, *September 1, 1939*

Contents

Daisy's Valentine

JOEY FELT THAT his romance with Daisy might ruin his life, but that didn't stop him. He liked the idea in fact. It had been a long time since he'd felt his life was in danger of further ruin, and it was fun to think it was still possible.

He worked with Daisy in the clerical department of a filthy secondhand bookstore on the Lower East Side of Manhattan. The department was a square-tiled space between morose gray metal stacks of books and a dirty wall with thin white pipes running along the bottom of it. There were brown boxes of books everywhere, scatterings of paper, ashtrays, Styrofoam cups, broken chairs, the occasional flashing mouse. Customers roamed the boundaries of the area, searching for the exit. Daisy, who sat nearest the bordering aisle, was always leaving her desk to sweetly assist some baffled old man with a sweating face and cockeyed glasses.

Joey's desk was a bare diagonal yard from Daisy's, and he would pace from there to the watercooler staring at her, rattling the epilepsy identification plates he wore around his neck and sighing. Then he would sit at his desk and shoot rubber bands at her. She usually wouldn't notice what he was doing until he'd surrounded her typewriter with red rubber squiggles. She'd look up and smile in her soft, dopey way, and continue shuffling papers with slow, long-fingered movements.

He had watched Daisy for almost a year before making a pass at her. He had been living with Diane for eight years and was reluctant to change anything that stable. Besides, he loved Diane. They'd had such a good eight years that by now it was almost a system.

He had met Diane at Bennington. He'd been impressed by her reputation in the art department, by the quality of the LSD she sold and by her rudeness. She was a tall, handsome thirty-three-year-old woman with taut, knit-together shoulders, and was so tense that her muscles were held scrunched together all the time. As a result, she was very muscular, even though she didn't do anything but lie around the loft and take drugs. He supported her by working in the bookstore as an accountant and by selling drugs. She helped out with the government checks she received as a certified mentally ill person.

They got high on Dexedrine for three and a half days out of the week. They'd been doing it religiously the whole time they'd been together. On Thursday morning, Joey's first working day, they would start. Joey would work at the store all day, and then come home and work on projects. He would take apart his computer and spread it all over the floor in small gray lumps. He would squat and play with the piles for hours before he'd put it back together. He'd do other things too. He once took a series of blue-and-white photos of the cow skeleton they had in the living room. He'd make tapes of noises that he thought sounded nice together. He'd program the computer. Sometimes he would just take his wind-up toys out of the toy chest and run them around while he listened to records. In the past, Diane would work on her big blobby paintings. By Sunday the loft floor would be scattered with wax papers covered with splotches of acrylic paint, sprayed with water and running together in dull purple streams. She used to work on a painting for months and then destroy it. Now she didn't paint at all. Instead she used her staying-up time to watch TV, walk the dogs or work out biorhythm charts on the computer.

On Sunday Joey would come home from work with bags under his eyes and his tendons standing out in funny ways. Diane would have two small salads ready in matching red bowls that her grandmother had given her. There would always be a moist radish neatly sliced and split apart on the top. They would eat the salad and go to sleep until Monday night. Then Diane would order sushi from the Japanese take-out place on the corner and arrange it on a long wooden chopping block when it came. They would cover it with salt and lemon and eat it with their fingers. Sometimes people would come over to buy drugs and they would play them records and chat. Then they would sleep. By Thursday morning they would be refreshed and ready to stay awake again until Sunday.

They made love about once a month. It didn't last long because they both thought it was monotonous and because Diane was disgusted by most of the things people do to stretch it out longer. However, when Joey started to think about Daisy he stopped making romantic advances to Diane at all, and she resented it.

She resented other things too. She was annoyed by his wind-up toys. If he left them out on the floor, she'd kick them. She didn't like the frozen pecan rolls he ate on Wednesday morning. She would complain about how revolting they looked, and then eat half of them.

Daisy was living with somebody too, but she ran around the bookstore babbling about her unfaithfulness as if it were the only thing she had to talk about. He liked to watch her pattering from desk to desk in her white sneakers, her jeans rasping softly between her small thighs with each narrow stride. She had to know what Evelyn and Ariel and everyone else around her thought about so-and-so not calling when he said he would. Then she wanted to know what they thought of her calling him and swearing at him. Or something like that. Her supervisor, Tommy, tolerated her because he was the kind of gay man who liked to hear about girls' romantic problems. He disapproved of her running around behind her boyfriend's back, but he enjoyed having the chance to moralize each time some new man dragged her through the dirt, as she put it. Daisy would say, "Tommy, I'm trying to make him leave. He won't go. I can't do anything about it."

Joey had once heard Tommy admit to another supervisor that Daisy was a terrible worker. "But she's a very special case," said Tommy. "I'd never fire her. What else could she do?"

Joey felt a pang of incredulous affection. Could she actually be less competent than the other bums in the typing pool? Everyone in it was a bad worker, except Evelyn. Evelyn was the only other girl there. She was an energetic, square-jawed woman who would type eighty words a minute. She wore tight jeans and cowboy shirts and thick black eyeliner that gathered in blobs in the corners of her eyes. Her streaked blond hair hung in her face and made her look masked and brutal. She had a collection of books about various mass murderers on her desk, and she could tell you all their personal histories.

The other three typists were fat, morose homosexuals who sat at their desks and ate from bags of cookies and complained. They had worked in the bookstore for years and they all talked desperately of "getting out." Ariel had been around the longest. He was six feet three inches tall and had round, demure shoulders, big hips and square fleshy breasts that embarrassed him. He had a small head, a long, bumpy nose and large brown eyes that were by turns sweetly candid or forlorn, but otherwise had a disturbing blank quality. He had enjoyed a brief notoriety in punk rock circles for his electric piano music. He talked about his past success in a meek, wistful voice, and showed people old pictures of himself dressed in black, wearing black wing-tipped sunglasses. He was terribly sensitive, and Tommy took advantage of his sensitivity to make fun of him. "Ariel is the spirit of the typing pool," Tommy would chatter as he ran from clerk to clerk with stacks of papers. "Whenever any of you are craving inspiration, just gaze on Ariel."

"Please, Tom, I'm on the verge of tears," Ariel would answer funereally.

"That's exactly what I'm talking about!" Tommy would scream.

When Joey first noticed Daisy, he wondered why this pretty young woman had chosen to work in a filthy, broken-down store amid unhappy homosexuals. As time went on, it seemed less and less inappropriate. She was comfortable in the typing pool. She was happy to listen to the boys talk about their adventures in leather bars, where men got blow jobs in open wooden booths or pissed on other men. She told jokes about Helen Keller and sex. She talked about her boyfriends and her painting. She was always crouching at Evelyn's desk, whispering and laughing about something, or looking at Evelyn's back issues of *True Detective* magazine. She wore T-shirts with pictures of cartoon characters on them, and bright-colored pants. Her brown hair was bobbed in a soft curve that ended on either side of her high cheekbones. When she walked, her shoulders and long neck were erect in a busy, almost ducklike way, but her hips and waist were fluid and gently mobile.

The heterosexual men were always coming to stand by her desk and talk to her about their poetry or political ideas while she looked at them and nodded. Even the gay men developed a certain bravado in her presence. Tommy kept on reassuring her that her prince was just around the corner. "I can feel it, Daisy," he would say exultantly. "You're on a collision course with Mr. Right!"

"Do you really think so, Tom?"

"It's obvious! Aren't you excited?"

Then Ariel would get up from his desk and lumber over to her and, bending from the waist, would put his large fleshy arms around her shoulders. Joey could see her small white hand emerge on Ariel's broad flank as she patiently patted him.

And, as if it weren't enough to be the heartthrob of the basement crowd, she was kind to helpless, repulsive people. There was a grotesque old woman who would come into the store from time to time to seek out her kindness. The woman was at least sixty years old, and covered her face with heavy orange makeup. She bought horrible best-sellers and self-help books with lurid red covers. She'd stand by Daisy's desk for half an hour and talk to her about how depressed she was. Daisy would turn off her typewriter and turn toward the woman with her chin in her hand. She'd listen gravely, agreeing sometimes, letting the woman give her small bags of hard candy and kiss her on the cheek. Everyone made rude comments about Daisy and "that crazy old dyke." But Daisy remained courteous and attentive to the distressed creature, even though she often made fun of her after she left.

Joey didn't think of having sex with Daisy, at least not in detail. It was more the idea of being near her, protecting her. She was obviously so confused. She looked everywhere for answers, for someone to tell her what to think. "I just want your perspective," she'd say.

There was a customer she called the "answer man" because he claimed that he could predict the future through "automatic handwriting." He was a handsome elderly man who wore expensive suits and looked as though he'd had at least one face lift. He had been coming into the store for years. Every time he came in, Daisy would walk him off into a corner and ask him questions. He would scrawl down answers in thin red ink and hand them to her with an imperious, terribly personal look. She would become either stricken or joyous. Later she would run around talking about what he'd said, examining the red-scrawled pieces of store stationery. "He says my painting is going to start being successful in a year and a half." "He says there are no worthwhile men around me and that there won't be for months." "He says David will move out next month."

"You don't take that stuff seriously, do you?" asked Joey.

"Oh, not really," she said. "But it's interesting." She went back to her desk and stuck the papers in her drawer and began typing, her face still glowing and upturned because someone who was possibly crazy had told her that she would eventually be a success.

He began thinking about her at home. He thought of her body resting against his, of his arm around her. He thought of her dressed in a white kimono, peeking from behind a fan, her eye makeup crinkling when she smiled. Diane became suspicious.

"You're a thousand miles away," she said over the Sunday salad. "What is it?"

"I'm preoccupied." His tone made it clear that her plaintiveness was futile, and she became frightened and angry. She didn't say anything, which was what he wanted.

He did not lie down with her that evening, although he was exhausted. He walked around the loft, striking the furniture with Diane's riding crop, annoying the cats, making them skitter across the floor, their eyes unnerved, their tails ruffled. His eyes dried in their sockets. His back was sore and balled into knots from staying up for three days.

He began doing things to attract Daisy's attention. He told jokes. He slapped his face with eau de toilette. He wore red pants and a sheathed knife in his belt. He did full splits and handstands. He talked about his active role in the theater department at Bennington and his classes with André Gregory. He mentioned the karate class he'd taken once, and punched a hole in a box of books. She said, "Joey has done everything!" There was a thrilling note of triumph in her voice.

For a long time he just looked at her. That alone made him so happy, he was afraid to try anything else. Maybe it would be better to hold her winglike shadow safe in the lock of his memory than to touch the breathing girl and lose her.

He decided to give her a card on Valentine's Day.

He spent days searching for the valentine material. He found what he wanted in an old illustrated children's book. It was a faded watercolor drawing of three red poppies sharing a field with pink clover and some blameless little weeds. A honey-colored bee with dreamily closed eyes was climbing a stalk. An aqua-green grasshopper was flying through a fuzzy, failing blue sky, its eyes blissfully shut, its hairy front legs dangling foolishly, its hind legs kicking, exultant, through the air. It was a distorted, feverish little drawing. The colors were all wrong. It made him think of paradise.

He tore it from the book and covered it with a piece of fragile paper so that the scene, veiled by the yellowing tissue haze, became remote and mysterious. He drew five hearts in misshapen lines and senselessly alternating sizes on the bottom of it. He colored them red. He wrote *"Voici le temps des assassins"* under them.

He carried it to work with him for several days before and after Valentine's Day. He decided dozens of times to give it to her, and changed his mind every time. He examined it daily, wondering if it was good enough. When he decided it was perfect, he thought perhaps it would be better to keep it in his drawer, where he alone knew it existed for her.

Finally, he said, "I have a valentine for you."

She pattered around his desk, smiling greedily. "Where is it?"

"In my drawer. I don't want to give it to you yet."

"Why not? Valentine's Day was a week ago. Can't I have it now?" She put her fingers on his shoulders like soft claws. "Give it to me now."

When he handed it to her, she hugged him and pressed against him. He giggled and put his arm around her. He sadly let go of his shadow captive.

That night he couldn't eat his spinach salad. The radish, gaily flowering red and white, was futile enticement. Diane sat across from him, stonily working her jaws. She sat rigidly straight-backed, her throat drawn so taut it looked as if it would be hard for her to swallow. He picked at the salad, turning the clean leaves this way and that. He stared past her, sighing, his dry eyes hot in their sockets.

"You look like an idiot," she said.

"I am."

The next day he took Daisy out to lunch, although he couldn't eat. He ordered a salad, which appeared in a beige plastic bowl. It was littered with pale carrot curls and flats of radish that accused him. He ignored it. He watched her eat from her dish of green and white cold noodles. They were curly and glistened with oil, and were garnished with bright pieces of slippery meat and vegetables. Daisy speared them serenely, three curls at a time.

"You can't imagine how wonderful this is for me," he said. "I've watched you for so long."

She smiled, he thought, uncertainly.

"You're so soft and gentle. You're like a delicate white flower."

"No, I'm not."

"I know you're probably not. But you seem like it, and that's good enough for me."

"What about Diane?"

"I'll leave Diane."

She put down her fork and stared at him. The chewing movement of her jaws was earnest and sweet. He smiled at her.

She swallowed, a neat, thorough swallow. "Don't leave Diane," she said.

"Why not? I love you."

"Oh, dear," she said. "This is getting out of hand. Why don't you eat your salad?"

"I can't. I'm medicated."

"You're what?"

He forced himself to eat the pale leaves and shreds of carrot.

They left the restaurant and walked around the block. Daisy butted her head against the harsh wind; her short gray coat floated in back of her like a sail. He held her mittened hand. "I love you," he said. "I don't care about anything else. I want to cast my mantle of protection over you."

"Let's sit here," she said. She sat down on an even rise of yellow brick in front of an apartment building that was an impression of yellow brick and shadowy gray glass shielding the sad blur of a doorman. He sat very near her and held her hand.

"I have to tell you some things about myself," she said. "I don't take admiration very well."

"I don't care if you take it well or not. It's there."

"But won't it make you unhappy if I don't return it?"

"I'd be disappointed, I guess. But I'd still have the pleasure of feeling it for you. It doesn't have to be returned." He wanted to put his hands on either side of her head and squeeze.

She looked at him intently. "I said that to someone recently," she said. "Do you suppose it's a trend of some kind?"

The wind blew away her bangs, baring her white forehead. He kissed the sudden openness. She dropped her head against his shoulder.

An old woman in a pink coating bearing a sequined flower with a disturbing burst of petals on her lapel looked at them and smiled. Her white face was heavy with wrinkles and pink makeup, and her smile seemed difficult under the weight. She sat on the short brick wall about two feet away from them.

"I'm not making myself clear," said Daisy. She lifted her head and looked at him with wide, troubled eyes. "If you're nice to me, I'll probably make you unhappy. I've done that to people."

"You couldn't make me unhappy."

"I'm only nice to people who are mostly mean to me. Once somebody told me to stay away from so-and-so because he beat up girls. They said he broke his girlfriend's jaw."

She paused, for emphasis, he supposed. The old lady was beginning to look depressed.

"So I began flirting with him like wild. Isn't that sick?"

"What happened?" asked Joey with interest.

"Nothing. He went to Bellevue before anything could. But isn't it awful? I actually wanted this nut to hit me." She paused again. "Aren't you disgusted?"

"Oh, I don't know."

The old lady rose slowly, head down, and walked away with stiff, painful steps. Her coat blew open; her blue-veined legs were oddly pretty.

Daisy turned to watch her. "See," she said. "She's disgusted even if you aren't. We've ruined her day."

Every day after work, he walked Daisy to a corner two blocks away from her apartment so he wouldn't meet her boyfriend, David. There was a drugstore on the corner with colored perfume bottles nesting in fistfuls of crepe paper in the window. The druggist, a middle-aged man with a big stomach and a disappointed face, stood at the door and watched them say good-bye. It was a busy corner; traffic ran savagely in the street, and people stamped by, staring in different directions, clutching their packages, briefcases and huge, screaming radios, their faces concentrated but empty. Daisy was silent and frail as a cattail, her fuzzy black mitten in Joey's hand, her eyes anxiously scanning the street for David. She would say good-bye to him several times, but he would pull her back by her lapel as she turned to cross the street. After the second time he stopped her, she would sigh and look down, then begin to go through her pockets for scraps of unwanted paper, which she tore into snowflake pieces and scattered like useless messages in the garbage-jammed metal wastebasket under the street lamp, as if, trapped on the corner, she might as well do something useful, like clean her pockets.

That day, when he finally let her go, he stood for a moment

and watched her pat across the street, through the awful march of people. He walked half a block to a candy store with an orange neon sign, and bought several white bags of jelly beans. Then he caught a cab and rode home like a sultan. He ignored Diane's bitter stare as he walked through the living room and shut himself up in the bedroom with his jelly beans.

He thought of rescuing Daisy. She would be walking across the street, with that airy, unaware look on her face. A car would roar around a garbage-choked corner, she would freeze in its path, her pale face helpless as a crouching rabbit. From out of nowhere he would leap, sweeping her aside with one arm, knocking them both to the sidewalk, to safety, her head cushioned on his arm. Or she would be accosted by a hostile teenager who would grab her coat and push her against a wall. Suddenly he would attack. The punk's legs would fly crazily as Joey slammed him against a crumbling brick wall. "If you hurt her, I'll . . ."

He sighed happily and got another pill and a handful of jelly beans.

"My mother couldn't understand me or do anything for me," he said. "She thought she was doing the right thing."

"She sounds like a bitch," said Daisy.

"Oh, no. She did what she could, given the circumstances. She at least recognized that I far surpassed her in intelligence."

"Then why did she let her boyfriend beat you up?"

"He didn't beat me up. He was just a fat slob who got a thrill out of putting a twelve-year-old in a half nelson and then asking how it felt."

"He beat you up."

They were in a small, dark bar. It had floors and tables made of old creaking wood, and a half-moon window of heavy stained glass in one wall. The tables were clawed with knifemarks, the french fries were large and damp. The waitresses carried themselves like dinosaurs with ungainly little hands and had purple veins on their legs, even though they were young. They were friendly though, and they looked right at you.

Daisy and Joey came here for lunch and sat in the deep, high-backed booths. Joey didn't eat, and by now Daisy knew why. He drank and watched her eat her hamburger with measured bites.

"I still can't understand why she married that repulsive pig. I ask her and she says 'because he makes me feel stable and secure.'"

"He doesn't sound stable to me."

"I guess he was, compared to my father. But then Dad was usually too drunk to make it down the stairs without falling, let alone hold a job. I mean, you're talking about a guy who died in the nut ward singing 'Joey, Foey, Bo-Poey, Bananarama Oh-Boey.' Any asshole is stable compared to that. But Tom? At least my father had style. He wouldn't have been caught dead in those ugly Dacron things Tom wears."

Daisy leaned into the corner of the booth and looked at him solemnly.

"When she first told me over the phone that she was getting married to Uncle Tom, I was happy. At least I'd get to come home instead of staying with my Christian Scientist relatives who made me wear those retarded plaid pants to school."

"She never should have sent you away like that," said Daisy. She sat up and pulled her drink closer, latching on to the straw with a jerking motion of her lip.

"She thought it was the right thing to do after my father died. Only she never knew how much my relatives hated me."

"I don't know how she could've thought it was the right thing to let him throw you out of the house when you were sixteen."

"He didn't throw me out. I just knew the constant fighting over whether or not I was a faggot was hurting my mother. I realized that I was more of an adult than they were and that it was up to me to change the situation."

Daisy leaned back with both hands on her glass as she sucked the straw, her cheeks palpitating gently. There were dainty gurgle noises coming from the bottom of her glass as she slurped the last of her drink. He smiled and took her hand. She squeezed his fingers. He gulped his alcohol, his pulse beating wildly to and fro. He hadn't really been thrown out of the house when he was sixteen. He had been eighteen when Tom went berserk at the sight of his anti-Vietnam poster and broke his nose.

Daisy put her glass on the table with a slurred movement. She leaned against him. He cradled her head and ordered more drinks.

"They couldn't believe it when I got that scholarship to Bennington. I didn't even tell them I applied. They already felt inferior to me."

"Did you drop out of college to get back at your mother?" Her voice was blurry from his shoulder.

"I dropped out because I couldn't stand the people. I couldn't stand the idea of art. Art is only good at the moment it's done. After that it's dead. It's just so much dead shit. Artists are like people trying to hoard their shit."

She sat away from him, reaching for her new glass. "I'm an artist. Diane is an artist. Why do you like us?"

He kissed the blue vein on her neck and enjoyed the silly beat of his heart. "You're like a pretty shadow."

Her eyes darted with worry. "You like me because I'm like you."

He smiled tolerantly and stroked her neck. "You're not like me. No one is like me. I'm a phenomenon."

She looked tired and turned away from him to her drink. "You're a misfit. So am I. We don't belong anywhere."

"Aww." He reached under her shirt and touched her small breast. She put her forehead against his neck, she put her hand between his legs. Her voice fluttered against his skin. "David has a gig out of town next week. Will you come stay with me?"

"Maybe."

Sometimes, though, he thought Daisy was sort of a stupid little thing. He thought it when he looked at Diane and noticed the stern, distinct line of her mouth, her strong nose, the muscles of her bared arms flexing as she furiously picked her nails. She didn't ask annoying questions about drugs. She never thought about being a misfit, or having a place in society. She loathed society. She sat still as a stone, her heavy-lidded eyes impassively half-closed, the inclination of her head in beautiful agreement with her lean, severe arm and the cigarette resting in her intelligent fingers.

But it was too late. Diane wouldn't talk to him anymore, except to insult him. She changed her medication days so she wouldn't be on schedule with him. Sometimes she didn't medicate at all. She said it made her cry.

He found her crying one day when he came home from work. It was so rare to see Diane cry that it was several minutes before he realized there were tears on her face. She was sitting in the aging purple armchair by the window, one leg drawn up and bent so that her knee shielded her face. Her shoulders were in a tight curl, she held her long bare foot tightly in her hand. She watched him walk past her. She let him reach the doorknob before she said, "You're seeing someone."

He stopped and faced her, thankful and relieved that she had said it first. "I meant to tell you," he said. "I didn't know how."

"You cowardly piece of shit."

"It's nothing serious," he said. "It's just an obsession."

"It's Daisy, isn't it?" She said the name like it was a disease.

"How did you know?"

"The way you mentioned her name. It was sickening."

"I didn't intend for it to happen."

"What a slime-bag you are."

It was then that he identified the glistening on her cheeks and chin. The tears were wrenching and poignant on her still face. He dropped his bag of jelly beans and moved toward her. He sat on the fat arm of the chair and put his arms around her rigid, shivering body. "I'm sorry," he said.

"It's like before," she said. "With Rita. It's so repulsive."

"If you can stay with me through this, just wait it out . . ."

"I want you out of here by the end of the month." The tears shimmered through her voice, which quivered like sunlight in a puddle. He wanted to make love to her.

"You're the cruelest person I've ever known." Her voice almost broke into panting. She yanked herself out of the chair and walked away, kicking the bag of jelly beans as she passed, spraying them across the floor. He waited until she was out of the room and then went to scoop up a handful of the red, orange and green ones. He ate them as he looked out the picture window and down into the street. There were two junkies in ugly jackets hunched beside the jagged hole in a wire fence. I am a slime-bag, he thought.

He went to his room to think about Daisy.

The next morning he went to Daisy's desk and sat near her on a box of books bearing an unflattering chalk drawing of the shipping department supervisor. She held her Styrofoam cup of tea with both hands and drank from it, looking over its rim with dark-shadowed eyes.

"She said I was the cruelest person she'd ever known."

"Oh, you're not so bad. She just doesn't get out of the house much. She doesn't know what's out there."

"You don't know me."

She put down her cup. "I talked to David last night. He cried too. He just lay there and stared at me with those big eyes. It was awful."

She picked up a piece of cardboard and began sweeping the mouse droppings on her desk into a neat pile. "So now they both know."

"And we can go to the opera tonight. I have tickets to *Die Walküre*. You can medicate and we can stay out all night."

"I don't want to medicate." She pulled the sticky, coffee-stained wastebasket out from under her desk and showered the mouse turds into it with a deft swish of cardboard.

Daisy had never been to an opera. "Will there be people in breast-plates and headdresses with horns?" she asked. "Will there be a papier-mâché dragon and things flying through the air?" She looked hard at the curtained stage.

"Probably not," he said. "I think this production is coming from a German Impressionist influence, which means they'll eschew costumes and scenery as much as possible. They're coming from an emphasis on symbolism and minimal design. It was a reaction against the earlier period when—"

"I want to see a dragon flying through the air." She took a pink mint from the box of opera mints he'd bought, popped it into her mouth and audibly sucked it. She shifted it to her cheek and asked, "Why do you like the opera?"

"I don't know, I like the music sometimes, I like to see how they put productions together. I like to watch the people."

"So do I."

"Sometimes I have this fantasy that the opera house is suddenly taken over by psychos or terrorists or something, and that I save everybody."

She stopped sucking her mint and turned to look at him. "How?"

"I jump from the balcony railing and scale down the curtain until I'm parallel with the cord. Then I jump for the cord, swing through the air—"

"That's impossible."

"Well, yes, I know. It's a fantasy."

"Why would you have a fantasy like that?" She looked disturbed.

"I don't know. It's not important."

She continued to stare at him, almost stricken. "I think it's because you feel estranged from people. You want something extreme to happen so you can show that you love them, and that you deserve love from them."

He pulled her head against his shoulder and kissed it. He said, "Sometimes I just want to tear you apart."

She put her box of mints in her lap and grabbed him tightly around the waist.

It was after midnight when they left the opera. They went to a neon-lit deli manned by aging waiters wearing red jackets, several of whom had violent tics in their jaws. Daisy persuaded him to order a salad and a milk shake; she was worried that he didn't eat enough. He sipped his shake uncomfortably and watched her eat cream cheese and salmon. She talked about her unhappy relationship with her father, pausing to bend her head so she could nip up the fallen croissant flakes with her tongue. Waiters ran around the table, some of them bearing three food-loaded plates in each hairy hand.

He tried to make her take some pills and stay out with him longer, but she said she felt too guilty about David. There was also some art work she wanted to do. She sighed and looked at the ground. She pulled away from him four times before he let her go. He watched her walk away and thought, "Now it's too late to buy jelly beans."

When he opened the door to his apartment, Diane hit him in the face. He was so startled, he stood there and let her hit him three more times before he grabbed her wrist.

"You filthy bastard!" she screamed. "You went to the opera with her! We always go to the opera together and you went with that cunt!"

"I hardly thought you wanted to go."

"Well, I did. I waited for you to come home from work." Her voice hobbled tearfully. "I never thought you would go with that cunt."

"She's not a cunt."

She swung her free hand, catching his ear. She yanked at the lobe, tearing out his tiny blue earring. It pinged on the floor, sparkled and rolled away. "Shit!" he screamed. He dropped to his knees and felt the floor with his palms. "Don't you have any self-control?"

"I don't give a shit about self-control. Get the fuck out."

"Will you just wait until I find my earring?"

"I don't care about your fucking earring. Get out before I kill you."

"God, you're so irrational."

He listened for sobbing from outside the slammed door. There was none. His ear was bleeding and his face burned, but he was oddly exhilarated. He was sorry Diane was so upset, but there was something stirring about a violent tantrum. It was the sort of thing he liked to tell stories about.

• • •

The street was buzzing with junkies and kids with big radios. They stood in a jumbled line against buildings and crawled out of holes in the walls and fences. They mumbled at him as he walked past. "I got the blues, I got the reds, I got the greens and blacks, the ones from last week."

He walked three blocks to Eliot's apartment; he didn't expect Eliot to answer the door, but he buzzed anyway. He was startled when Eliot's suspicious voice darted from the cluster of tiny holes that served as an intercom.

"It's the F.B.I.," said Joey.

There was a grudging silence before the buzzer squawked. When Joey reached the apartment door, Eliot poked his head out, one finger to his lips. His wispy brown hair stuck out in a ratty halo; his round, thin-lashed eyes were hysterically wide and moist. "Whatever you do, don't mention drugs," he whispered. "If you have to refer to them at all, say 'gum' or something. Only don't be conspicuous."

"All right," said Joey.

"They've got the place wired," explained Eliot. "We tore the apartment apart and we still can't find the bug. Are you sure you weren't followed?"

Joey nodded. Eliot stretched his neck and stared into the empty hall, blinking his damp eyes hard. Satisfied, he let Joey in.

Rita was lying on the couch in front of a partially dismantled TV screen with a soundless picture on it. Her large feet hung over the edge of the couch, her hands were limp at the ends of her thin, prominently veined wrists. Her head drooped sideways on her slender, listless neck, almost falling off the couch. When she saw Joey she lifted her head, and her dark eyes lighted.

He flapped his hand at her and sat on a hard-backed chair. "Diane threw me out of the house," he said.

"Yeah?" said Eliot. He got on his knees and began looking through the records scattered on the floor.

"It doesn't matter. I wanted to move anyway. I'm in love. It's all over between Diane and me."

"You should've made that decision five years ago," said Rita.

Eliot whirled around, waving a record. "You've got to hear this. It's the most incredible thing."

"Oh, Jesus Christ, that record came out ten years ago," said Rita. "Just because you've only heard it for the first time."

Eliot tore the record from its jacket, tossed the jacket across the room and knelt before the turntable. He lifted the needle and examined it, blowing delicately.

Rita threw her long legs up and sat with her small bony knees together, her feet toeing in. "Who are you in love with?"

"You know, she's still showing those stupid home movies of you in the bathtub," said Eliot. "She watches them and masturbates. It's hilarious. She shows them to everybody."

"Who is it?" asked Rita.

"This girl at the store named Daisy."

"Oh. I guess it figures." She leaned forward to the cluttered table for a match. Her dark hair fell across her face with the graceful motion of a folding wing. She leaned back, exposing her face again. The lines under her eyes were deep and black with smeared makeup. "Got any pills, Joe?"

Eliot jumped up. "Don't say that!" he screamed.

"Oh, you asshole," said Rita. "Got any . . . socks?"

"Sure." Joey poured a colorful tumble into her palm.

"What are you trying to do to me?" said Eliot through his teeth. "Are you working for them or what?"

Joey looked around; they really had torn up the apartment. Dead plants were turned over in their broken pots, slashed pillows spilled yellow foam out onto the floor, cardboard boxes lay with their lids yanked open, their contents exposed and strewn. The filing cabinet was tipped over, its open drawers freeing a white dance of paper. At least the broken bottles had been swept safely into piles.

Eliot's rare book collection was preserved in a prim stack beside the couch. Joey could see the three Bartolovs he'd sold him. Eliot had been awed when he'd discovered that Joey's pill connection was Alexander Bartolov, the famous poet.

"Oh, come on Rita, just a little blow job," said Eliot. "I won't come or anything."

"Forget it," said Rita. She lay back into the couch, her spidery white hand over her eyes. Her long limp legs recalled the flying grasshopper on Daisy's valentine.

"She's still hot for you, you know," said Eliot. "I still have to hear about the times you tied her up and spanked her."

"Can't we change the subject?" said Joey.

"Okay," said Eliot cheerfully. "I'm going to the bathroom anyway. I'm nauseous."

"Don't relax," said Rita. "He'll be back in a minute."

"It's all right with me," said Joey. He took a magazine off the table. It was open to a picture of a masked woman dressed in a red rubber suit that a man was inflating with a pump. On the next page, a naked girl was tied with belts in a kneeling position on a bathroom floor. An ornery-looking young fellow approached her from behind with a rubber hose; she looked over her shoulder, her lips parted in a look of coy fear. He was surprised at how pretty she was. Her cheekbones and shoulders were like Daisy's.

Daisy and Joey emerged from the movie theater holding hands. "We have no place to go," said Daisy. "It's been a month since we've been alone in a room. And David won't leave." They walked, still holding hands.

"I feel so terrible about David," she said. "He's such a lovely, innocent person. He's the purest person I know."

"There are no pure people."

"You haven't seen David. He has such naked eyes. When you touch him, it's like there's nothing between you and him." She looked at him quizzically. "You're not like that. When I touch you, I don't feel you at all."

"There's nothing to feel."

"Don't say that about yourself." She dropped his hand and rubbed his back with her mittened hand. "Anyway, it's good you're not like David. Even as you are, I worry about you being too nice to me."

He put his hand around her neck. "I don't know what makes you think I have any intention of being nice to you."

She turned and kissed him. He took a handful of her hair in his fist and pulled her head tautly back while he kissed her.

They sat on the cold stone steps of an apartment building. They unbuttoned their jackets and huddled together, his hands on either side of her softly sweatered body.

"You're so strange," she said. "It's hard to talk to you."

"How so?"

"You're always talking at me. You don't listen to what I say."

"I seem strange because I'm special."

"I think it's because you take so many pills."

"You should start taking them. Did you know the government gives them to soldiers who are about to go into combat? They sharpen the reflexes, senses, everything."

"I'm not going into combat."

There was a sound from above. They turned and saw a handsome, well-dressed middle-aged couple at the head of the steps. Joey saw a flicker of admiration in Daisy's face as she looked at the tall blond lady in her evening dress. The couple began to descend. Daisy and Joey stood and squeezed into a stony corner to let them pass. The man's shoulder scratched against Joey. The man coughed, quite unnecessarily.

"Excuse me," said the woman. "We only live here."

"You have plenty of room," said Daisy sharply.

"You have no business being here," said the man. The couple stood on the sidewalk and frowned, their shoulders indignant.

"Why do you care?" said Daisy. "We aren't in your way." Her voice quivered oddly.

"Ssssh," said Joey. "Let them live their lives."

"You are very rude," said the woman. "If you're here when we get back, we're going to call the police." She swept away, sweeping her husband with her. They were probably in a hurry.

Joey watched the woman's dress fluttering along the pavement. "That was strange," he said. "I've sat on lots of steps before and that's never happened."

Daisy didn't answer.

"I guess it's different in the East Village."

Daisy sniffed wetly.

He reached into his pocket and got out his bag of jelly beans. He offered some to Daisy, but she ignored him. Her head was down, and slow, quiet tears ran singly down her nose. He put his arms around her. "Hey, come on," he said. He felt no response from her. She didn't move or look at him.

He dropped his arm and looked away, confused. He ate his jelly beans and looked at the pool of lamplight in the black street.

A Romantic Weekend

S HE WAS MEETING a man she had recently and abruptly fallen in love with. She was in a state of ghastly anxiety. He was married, for one thing, to a Korean woman whom he described as the embodiment of all that was feminine and elegant. Not only that, but a psychic had told her that a relationship with him could cripple her emotionally for the rest of her life. On top of this, she was tormented by the feeling that she looked inadequate. Perhaps her body tilted too far forward as she walked, perhaps her jacket made her torso look bulky in contrast to her calves and ankles, which were probably skinny. She felt like an object unraveling in every direction. In anticipation of their meeting, she had not been able to sleep the night before; she had therefore eaten some amphetamines and these had heightened her feeling of disintegration.

When she arrived at the corner he wasn't there. She stood against a building, trying to arrange her body in the least repulsive configuration possible. Her discomfort mounted. She crossed the street and stood on the other corner. It seemed as though everyone who walked by was eating. A large, distracted businessman went by holding a half-eaten hot dog. Two girls passed, sharing cashews from a white bag. The eating added to her sense that the world was disorderly and unbeautiful. She became acutely aware of the garbage on the street. The wind stirred it; a candy wrapper waved forlornly from its trapped position in the mesh of a jammed public wastebasket. This was all wrong, all horrible. Her meeting with him should be perfect and scrap-free. She couldn't bear the thought of flapping trash. Why wasn't he there to meet her? Minutes passed. Her shoulders drew together.

She stepped into a flower store. The store was clean and white, except for a few smudges on the linoleum floor. Homosexuals with low voices stood behind the counter. Arranged stalks bearing absurd blossoms protruded from sedate round vases and bristled in the aisles. She had a paroxysm of fantasy. He held her, helpless and swooning, in his arms. They were supported by a soft ball of puffy blue stuff. Thornless roses surrounded their heads. His gaze penetrated her so thoroughly, it was as though he had thrust his hand into her chest and begun feeling her ribs one by one. This was all right with her. "I have never met anyone I felt this way about," he said. "I love you." He made her do things she'd never done before, and then they went for a walk and looked at the new tulips that were bound to have grown up somewhere. None of this felt stupid or corny, but she knew that it was. Miserably, she tried to gain a sense of proportion. She stared at the flowers. They were an agony of bright, organized beauty. She couldn't help it. She wanted to give him flowers. She wanted to be with him in a room full of flowers. She visualized herself standing in front of him, bearing a handful of blameless flowers trapped in the ugly pastel paper the florist would staple around them. The vision was brutally embarrassing, too much so to stay in her mind for more than seconds.

She stepped out of the flower store. He was not there. Her anxiety approached despair. They were supposed to spend the weekend together.

He stood in a cheap pizza stand across the street, eating a greasy slice and watching her as she stood on the corner. Her anxiety was visible to him. It was at once disconcerting and weirdly attractive. Her appearance otherwise was not pleasing. He couldn't quite put his finger on why this was. Perhaps it was the suggestion of meekness in her dress, of a desire to be inconspicuous, or worse, of plain thoughtlessness about how clothes looked on her.

He had met her at a party during the previous week. She immediately reminded him of a girl he had known years before, Sharon, a painfully serious girl with a pale, gentle face whom he had tormented off and on for two years before leaving for his wife. Although it had gratified him enormously to leave her, he had

missed hurting her for years, and had been half-consciously looking for another woman with a similarly fatal combination of pride,
weakness and a foolish lust for something resembling passion. On
meeting Beth, he was astonished at how much she looked, talked
and moved like his former victim. She was delicately morbid in all
her gestures, sensitive, arrogant, vulnerable to flattery. She veered
between extravagant outbursts of opinion and sudden, uncertain
halts, during which she seemed to look to him for approval. She
was in love with the idea of intelligence, and she overestimated her
own. Her sense of the world, though she presented it aggressively,
could be, he sensed, snatched out from under her with little or no
trouble. She said, "I hope you are a savage."

He went home with her that night. He lay with her on her sag-
ging, lumpy single mattress, tipping his head to blow smoke into
the room. She butted her forehead against his chest. The mattress
squeaked with every movement. He told her about Sharon. "I had
a relationship like that when I was in college," she said. "Somebody
opened me up in a way that I had no control over. He hurt me. He
changed me completely. Now I can't have sex normally."

The room was pathetically decorated with postcards, pictures
of huge-eyed Japanese cartoon characters, and tiny, maddening
toys that she had obviously gone out of her way to find, displayed
in a tightly arranged tumble on her dresser. A frail model airplane
dangled from the light above dresser. Next to it was a pasted-
up cartoon of a pink-haired girl cringing open-mouthed before
a spire-haired boy-villain in shorts and glasses. Her short skirt
was blown up by the force of his threatening expression, and her
panties showed. What kind of person would put crap like this up
on her wall?

"I'm afraid of you," she murmured.

"Why?"

"Because I just am."

"Don't worry. I won't give you any more pain than you can
handle."

She curled against him and squeezed her feet together like a
stretching cat. Her socks were thick and ugly, and her feet were

large for her size. Details like this could repel him, but he felt tenderly toward the long, grubby, squeezed-together feet. He said, "I want a slave."

She said, "I don't know. We'll see."

He asked her to spend the weekend with him three days later.

It had seemed like a good idea at the time, but now he felt an irritating combination of guilt and anxiety. He thought of his wife, making breakfast with her delicate, methodical movements, or in the bathroom, painstakingly applying kohl under her huge eyes, flicking away the excess with pretty, birdlike finger gestures, her thin elbows raised, her eyes blank with concentration. He thought of Beth, naked and bound, blind-folded and spread-eagled on the floor of her cluttered apartment. Her cartoon characters grinned as he beat her with a whip. Welts rose on her breasts, thighs, stomach and arms. She screamed and twisted, wrenching her neck from side to side. She was going to be scarred for life. He had another picture of her sitting across from him at a restaurant, very erect, one arm on the table, her face serious and intent. Her large glasses drew her face down, made it look somber and elegant. She was smoking a cigarette with slow, mournful intakes of breath. These images lay on top of one another, forming a hideously confusing grid. How was he going to sort them out? He managed to separate the picture of his wife and the original picture of blindfolded Beth and hold them apart. He imagined himself traveling happily between the two. Perhaps, as time went on, he could bring Beth home and have his wife beat her too. She would do the dishes and serve them dinner. The grid closed up again and his stomach went into a moil. The thing was complicated and potentially exhausting. He looked at the anxious girl on the corner. She had said that she wanted to be hurt, but he suspected that she didn't understand what that meant.

He should probably just stay in the pizza place and watch her until she went away. It might be entertaining to see how long she waited. He felt a certain pity for her. He also felt, from his glassed-in vantage point, as though he were torturing an insect. He gloated as he ate his pizza.

At the height of her anxiety she saw him through the glass wall of the pizza stand. She immediately noticed his gloating countenance. She recognized the coldly scornful element in his watching and waiting as opposed to greeting her. She suffered, but only for an instant; she was then smitten by love. She smiled and crossed the street with a senseless confidence in the power of her smile.

"I was about to come over," he said. "I had to eat first. I was starving." He folded the last of his pizza in half and stuck it in his mouth.

She noticed a piece of bright orange pizza stuck between his teeth, and it endeared him to her.

They left the pizza stand. He walked with wide steps, and his heavy black overcoat swung rakishly, she thought, above his boots. He was a slight, slender boy with a pale, narrow face and blond hair that wisped across one brow. In the big coat he looked like the young pet of a budding secret police force. She thought he was beautiful.

He hailed a cab and directed the driver to the airport. He looked at her sitting beside him. "This is going to be a disaster," he said. "I'll probably wind up leaving you there and coming back alone."

"I hope not," she said. "I don't have any money. If you left me there, I wouldn't be able to get back by myself."

"That's too bad. Because I might." He watched her face for a reaction. It showed discomfort and excitement and something that he could only qualify as foolishness, as if she had just dropped a tray full of glasses in public. "Don't worry, I wouldn't do that," he said. "But I like the idea that I could."

"So do I." She was terribly distressed. She wanted to throw her arms around him.

He thought: There is something wrong. Her passivity was pleasing, as was her silence and her willingness to place herself in his hands. But he sensed another element present in her that he could not define and did not like. Her tightly folded hands were nervous and repulsive. Her public posture was brittle, not pliant. There was a rigidity that if cracked would yield nothing. He was disconcerted to realize that he didn't know if he could crack it anyway. He began to feel uncomfortable. Perhaps the weekend would be a disaster.

They arrived at the airport an hour early. They went to a bar and drank. The bar was an open-ended cube with a red neon sign that said "Cocktails." There was no sense of shelter in it. The furniture was spindly and exposed, and there were no doors to protect you from the sight of dazed, unattractive passengers wandering through the airport with their luggage. She ordered a Bloody Mary.

"I can't believe you ordered that," he said.

"Why not?"

"Because I want a bloody Beth." He gave her a look that made her think of a neurotic dog with its tongue hanging out, waiting to bite someone.

"Oh," she said.

He offered her a cigarette.

"I don't smoke," she said. "I told you twice."

"Well, you should start."

They sat quietly and drank for several minutes.

"Do you like to look at people?" she asked.

She was clearly struggling to talk to him. He saw that her face had become very tense. He could've increased her discomfort, but for the moment he had lost the energy to do so. "Yes," he said. "I do."

They spent some moments regarding the people around them. They were short on material. There were only a few customers in the bar; most of them were men in suits who sat there seemingly enmeshed in a web of habit and accumulated rancor that they called their personalities, so utterly unaware of their entanglement that they clearly considered themselves men of the world, even though they had long ago stopped noticing it. Then a couple walked through the door, carrying luggage. The woman's bright skirt flashed with each step. The man walked ahead of her. He walked too fast for her to keep up. She looked harried. Her eyes were wide and dark and clotted with makeup; there was a mole on her chin. He paused, as though considering whether he would stop for a drink. He decided not to and strode again. Her earrings jiggled as she followed. They left a faint trail of sex and disappointment behind them.

Beth watched the woman's hips move under her skirt. "There was something unpleasant about them," she said.

"Yes, there was."

It cheered her to find this point of contact. "I'm sorry I'm not more talkative," she said.

"That's all right." His narrow eyes became feral once again. "Women should be quiet." It suddenly struck her that it would seem completely natural if he lunged forward and bit her face.

"I agree," she said sharply. "There aren't many men around worth talking to."

He was nonplussed by her peevish tone. Perhaps, he thought, he'd imagined it.

He hadn't.

They had more drinks on the plane. They were served a hunk of white-frosted raisin pastry in a red paper bag. He wasn't hungry, but the vulgar cake appealed to him so he stuck it in his baggage.

They had a brief discussion about shoes, from the point of view of expense and aesthetics. They talked about intelligence and art. There were large gaps of silence that were disheartening to both of them. She began talking about old people, and how nice they could be. He had a picture of her kneeling on the floor in black stockings and handcuffs. This picture became blurred, static-ridden, and then obscured by their conversation. He felt a ghastly sense of longing. He called back the picture, which no longer gave him any pleasure. He superimposed it upon a picture of himself standing in a nightclub the week before, holding a drink and talking to a rather combative girl who wanted his number.

"Some old people are beautiful in an unearthly way," she continued. "I saw this old lady in the drugstore the other day who must've been in her nineties. She was so fragile and pretty, she was like a little elf."

He looked at her and said, "Are you going to start being fun to be around or are you going to be a big drag?"

She didn't answer right away. She didn't see how this followed her comment about the old lady. "I don't know."

"I don't think you're very sexual," he said. "You're not the way I thought you were when I first met you."

She was so hurt by this that she had difficulty answering. Finally, she said, "I can be very sexual or very unsexual depending on who I'm with and in what situation. It has to be the right kind of thing. I'm sort of a cerebral person. I think I respond to things in a cerebral way, mostly."

"That's what I mean."

She was struck dumb with frustration. She had obviously disappointed him in some fundamental way, which she felt was completely due to misunderstanding. If only she could think of the correct thing to say, she was sure she could clear it up. The blue puffball thing unfurled itself before her with sickening power. It was the same image of him holding her and gazing into her eyes with bone-dislodging intent, thinly veiling the many shattering events that she anticipated between them. The prospect made her disoriented with pleasure. The only problem was, this image seemed to have no connection with what was happening now. She tried to think back to the time they had spent in her apartment, when he had held her and said, "You're cute." What had happened between then and now to so disappoint him?

She hadn't yet noticed how much he had disappointed her.

He couldn't tell if he was disappointing her or not. She completely mystified him, especially after her abrupt speech on cerebralism. It was now impossible to even have a clear picture of what he wanted to do to this unglamorous creature, who looked as though she bit her nails and read books at night. Dim, half-formed pictures of his wife, Sharon, Beth and a sixteen-year-old Chinese hooker he'd seen a month before crawled aimlessly over each other. He sat and brooded in a bad-natured and slightly drunken way.

She sat next to him, diminished and fretful, with idiot radio songs about sex in her head.

• • •

They were staying in his grandmother's deserted apartment in Washington, D.C. The complex was a series of building blocks seemingly arranged at random, stuck together and painted the least attractive colors available. It was surrounded by bright green grass and a circular driveway, and placed on a quiet highway that led into the city. There was a drive-in bank and an insurance office next to it. It was enveloped in the steady, continuous noise of cars driving by at roughly the same speed.

"This is a horrible building," she said as they traveled up in the elevator.

The door slid open and they walked down a hall carpeted with dense brown nylon. The grandmother's apartment opened before them. Beth found the refrigerator and opened it. There was a crumpled package of French bread, a jar of hot peppers, several lumps covered with aluminum foil, two bottles of wine and a six-pack. "Is your grandmother an alcoholic?" she asked.

"I don't know." He dropped his heavy leather bag and her white canvas one in the living room, took off his coat and threw it on the bags. She watched him standing there, pale and gaunt in a black leather shirt tied at his waist with a leather belt. That image of him would stay with her for years for no good reason and with no emotional significance. He dropped into a chair, his thin arms flopping lightly on its arms. He nodded at the tray of whiskey, Scotch and liqueurs on the coffee table before him. "Why don't you make yourself a drink?"

She dropped to her knees beside the table and nervously played with the bottles. He was watching her quietly, his expression hooded. She plucked a bottle of thick chocolate liqueur from the cluster, poured herself a glass and sat in the chair across from his with both hands around it. She could no longer ignore the character of the apartment. It was brutally ridiculous, almost sadistic in its absurdity. The couch and chairs were covered with a floral print. A thin maize carpet zipped across the floor. There were throw rugs. There were artificial flowers. There was an abundance of small tables and shelves housing a legion of figures; grinning glass maidens in sumptuous gowns bore baskets of glass roses, ceramic birds warbled from the ceramic stumps they clung to, glass horses galloped across teakwood pastures. A ceramic weather poodle and his diamond-eyed kitty-cat companions silently watched the silent scene in the room.

"Are you all right?" he asked.

"I hate this apartment. It's really awful."

"What were you expecting? Jesus Christ. It's a lot like yours, you know."

"Yes. That's true, I have to admit." She drank her liqueur.

"Do you think you could improve your attitude about this whole thing? You might try being a little more positive."

Coming from him, this question was preposterous. He must be so pathologically insecure that his perception of his own behavior was thoroughly distorted. He saw rejection everywhere, she decided; she must reassure him. "But I do feel positive about being here," she said. She paused, searching for the best way to express the extremity of her positive feelings. She invisibly implored him to see and mount their blue puffball bed. "It would be impossible for you to disappoint me. The whole idea of you makes me happy. Anything you do will be all right."

Her generosity unnerved him. He wondered if she realized what she was saying. "Does anybody know you're here?" he asked. "Did you tell anyone where you were going?"

"No." She had in fact told several people.

"That wasn't very smart."

"Why not?"

"You don't know me at all. Anything could happen to you."

She put her glass on the coffee table, crossed the floor and dropped to her knees between his legs. She threw her arms around his thighs. She nuzzled his groin with her nose. He tightened. She unzipped his pants. "Stop," he said. "Wait." She took his shoulders—she had a surprisingly strong grip—and pulled him to the carpet. His hovering brood of images and plans was suddenly upended, as though it had been sitting on a table that a rampaging crazy person had flipped over. He felt assaulted and invaded. This was not what he had in mind, but to refuse would make him seem somehow less virile than she. Queasily, he stripped off her clothes and put their bodies in a viable position. He fastened his teeth on her breast and bit her. She made a surprised noise and her body stiffened. He bit her again, harder. She screamed. He wanted to draw blood. Her screams were short and stifled. He could tell that she was trying to like being bitten, but that she did not. He gnawed her breast. She screamed sharply. They screwed. They broke apart and regarded each other warily. She put her hand on his tentatively. He realized what had been disturbing him about her. With other women whom he had been with in similar situations, he had experienced a relaxing sense of emptiness within them that had made it easy for him to get inside them and, once there, smear himself all over their innermost territory until it was no longer theirs but his. His wife did not have this empty quality, yet the gracious way in which she emptied herself for him made her submission, as far as it went, all the more poignant. This exasperating girl, on the other hand, contained a tangible something-thingness that she not only refused to expunge, but that seemed to willfully expand itself so that he banged into it with every attempt to invade her. He didn't mind the somethingness; he rather liked it, in fact, and had looked forward to seeing it demolished. But she refused to let him do it. Why had she told him she was a masochist? He looked at her body. Her limbs were muscular and alert. He considered taking her by the neck and bashing her head against the floor.

He stood abruptly. "I want to get something to eat. I'm starving."

She put her hand on his ankle. Her desire to abase herself had been completely frustrated. She had pulled him to the rug certain that if only they could fuck, he would enter her with overwhelming force and take complete control of her. Instead she had barely felt him, and what she had felt was remote and cold. Somewhere on her exterior he'd been doing some biting thing that meant nothing to her and was quite unpleasant. Despairing, she held his ankle tighter and put her forehead on the carpet. At least she could stay at his feet, worshiping. He twisted free and walked away. "Come on," he said.

The car was in the parking lot. It was because of the car that this weekend had come about. It was his wife's car, an expensive thing that her ex-husband had given her. It had been in Washington for over a year; he was here to retrieve it and drive it back to New York.

Beth was appalled by the car. It was a loud yellow monster with a narrow, vicious shape and absurd doors that snapped up from the roof and out like wings. In another setting it might have seemed glamorous, but here, behind this equally monstrous building, in her unsatisfactory clothing, the idea of sitting in it with him struck her as comparable to putting on a clown nose and wearing it to dinner.

They drove down a suburban highway lined with small businesses, malls and restaurants. It was twilight; several neon signs blinked consolingly.

"Do you think you could make some effort to change your mood?" he said.

"I'm not in a bad mood," she said wearily. "I just feel blank."

Not blank enough, he thought.

He pulled into a Roy Rogers fast food cafeteria. She thought: He is not even going to take me to a nice place. She was insulted. It seemed as though he was insulting her on purpose. The idea was incredible to her.

She walked through the line with him, but did not take any of the shiny dishes of food displayed on the fluorescent-lit aluminum shelves. He felt a pang of worry. He was no longer angry, and her drawn white face disturbed him.

"Why aren't you eating?"

"I'm not hungry."

They sat down. He picked at his food, eyeing her with veiled alarm. It occurred to her that it might embarrass him to eat in front of her while she ate nothing. She asked if she could have some of his salad. He eagerly passed her the entire bowl of pale leaves strewn with orange dressing. "Have it all."

He huddled his shoulders orphanlike as he ate; his blond hair stood tangled like pensive weeds. "I don't know why you're not eating," he said fretfully. "You're going to be hungry later on."

Her predisposition to adore him was provoked. She smiled.

"Why are you staring at me like that?" he asked.

"I'm just enjoying the way you look. You're very airy."

Again, his eyes showed alarm.

"Sometimes when I look at you, I feel like I'm seeing a tank of small, quick fish, the bright darting kind that go every which way."

He paused, stunned and dangle-forked over his pinched, curled-up steak. "I'm beginning to think you're out of your fucking mind."

Her happy expression collapsed.

"Why can't you talk to me in a half-normal fucking way?" he continued. "Like the way we talked on the plane. I liked that. That was a conversation." In fact, he hadn't liked the conversation on the plane either, but compared to this one, it seemed quite all right.

When they got back to the apartment, they sat on the floor and drank more alcohol. "I want you to drink a lot," he said. "I want to make you do things you don't want to do."

"But I won't do anything I don't want to do. You have to make me want it."

He lay on his back in silent frustration.

"What are your parents like?" she asked.

"What?"

"Your parents. What are they like?"

"I don't know. I don't have that much to do with them. My mother is nice. My father's a prick. That's what they're like." He put one hand over his face; a square-shaped album-style view of his family presented itself. They were all at the breakfast table, talking and reaching for things. His mother moved in the background, a slim, worried shadow in her pink robe. His sister sat next to him, tall, blond and arrogant, talking and flicking at toast crumbs in the corners of her mouth. His father sat at the head of the table, his big arms spread over everything, leaning over his plate as if he had to defend it, gnawing his breakfast. He felt unhappy and then angry. He thought of a little Italian girl he had met in a go-go bar a while back, and comforted himself with the memory of her slim haunches and pretty high-heeled feet on either side of his head as she squatted over him.

"It seems that way with my parents when you first look at them. But in fact my mother is much more aggressive and, I would say, more cruel than my father, even though she's more passive and soft on the surface."

She began a lengthy and, in his view, incredible and unnecessary history of her family life, including descriptions of her brother and sister. Her entire family seemed to have a collectively disturbed personality characterized by long brooding silences, unpleasing compulsive sloppiness (unflushed toilets, used Kleenex abandoned everywhere, dirty underwear on the floor) and outbursts of irrational, violent anger. It was horrible. He wanted to go home.

He poked himself up on his elbows. "Are you a liar?" he asked. "Do you lie often?"

She stopped in midsentence and looked at him. She seemed to consider the question earnestly. "No," she said. "Not really. I mean, I can lie, but I usually don't about important things. Why do you ask?"

"Why did you tell me you were a masochist?"

"What makes you think I'm not?"

"You don't act like one."

"Well, I don't know how you can say that. You hardly know me. We've hardly done anything yet."

"What do you want to do?"

"I can't just come out and tell you. It would ruin it."

He picked up his cigarette lighter and flicked it, picked up her shirt and stuck the lighter underneath. She didn't move fast enough. She screamed and leapt to her feet.

"Don't do that! That's awful!"

He rolled over on his stomach. "See. I told you. You're not a masochist."

"Shit! That wasn't erotic in the least. I don't come when I stub my toe either."

In the ensuing silence it occurred to her that she was angry, and had been for some time.

"I'm tired," she said. "I want to go to bed." She walked out of the room.

He sat up. "Well, we're making decisions, aren't we?"

She reentered the room. "Where are we supposed to sleep, anyway?"

He showed her the guest room and the fold-out couch. She immediately began dismantling the couch with stiff, angry movements. Her body seemed full of unnatural energy and purpose. She had, he decided, ruined the weekend, not only for him but for herself. Her willful, masculine, stupid somethingness had obstructed their mutual pleasure and satisfaction. The only course of action left was hostility. He opened his grandmother's writing desk and took out a piece of paper and a Magic Marker. He wrote the word "stupid" in thick black letters. He held it first near her chest, like a placard, and then above her crotch. She ignored him.

"Where are the sheets?" she asked.

"How'd you get so tough all of a sudden?" He threw the paper on the desk and took a sheet from a dresser drawer.

"We'll need a blanket too, if we open the window. And I want to open the window."

He regarded her sarcastically. "You're just keeping yourself from getting what you want by acting like this."

"You obviously don't know what I want."

They got undressed. He contemptuously took in the mascular, energetic look of her body. She looked more like a boy than a girl, in spite of her pronounced hips and round breasts. Her short, spiky red hair was more than enough to render her masculine. Even the dark bruise he had inflicted on her breast and the slight burn from his lighter failed to lend her a more feminine quality.

She opened the window. They got under the blanket on the fold-out couch and lay there, not touching, as though they really were about to sleep. Of course, neither one of them could.

"Why is this happening?" she asked.

"You tell me."

"I don't know. I really don't know." Her voice was small and pathetic.

"Part of it is that you don't talk when you should, and then you talk too much when you shouldn't be saying anything at all."

In confusion, she reviewed the various moments they had spent together, trying to classify them in terms of whether or not it had been appropriate to speak, and to rate her performance accordingly. Her confusion increased. Tears floated on her eyes. She curled her body against his.

"You're hurting my feelings," she said, "but I don't think you're doing it on purpose."

He was briefly touched. "Accidental pain," he said musingly. He took her head in both hands and pushed it between his legs. She opened her mouth compliantly. He had hurt her after all, he reflected. She was confused and exhausted, and at this instant, anyway, she was doing what he wanted her to do. Still, it wasn't enough. He released her and she moved upward to lie on top of him, resting her head on his shoulder. She spoke dreamily. "I would do anything with you."

"You would not. You would be disgusted."

"Disgusted by what?"

"You would be disgusted if I even told you."

She rolled away from him. "It's probably nothing."

"Have you ever been pissed on?"

He gloated as he felt her body tighten.

"No."

"Well, that's what I want to do to you."

"On your grandmother's rug?"

"I want you to drink it. If any got on the rug, you'd clean it up."

"Oh."

"I knew you'd be shocked."

"I'm not. I just never wanted to do it."

"So? That isn't any good to me."

In fact, she was shocked. Then she was humiliated, and not in the way she had planned. Her seductive puffball cloud deflated with a flaccid hiss, leaving two drunken, bad-tempered, incompetent, malodorous people blinking and uncomfortable on its remains. She stared at the ugly roses with their heads collapsed in a dead wilt and slowly saw what a jerk she'd been. Then she got mad.

"Do you like people to piss on you?" she asked.

"Yeah. Last month I met this great girl at Billy's Topless. She pissed in my face for only twenty bucks."

His voice was high-pitched and stupidly aggressive, like some weird kid who would walk up to you on the street and offer to take care of your sexual needs. How, she thought miserably, could she have mistaken this hostile moron for the dark, brooding hero who would crush her like an insect and then talk about life and art?

"There's a lot of other things I'd like to do too," he said with odd self-righteousness. "But I don't think you could handle it."

"It's not a question of handling it." She said these last two words very sarcastically. "So far everything you've said to me has been incredibly banal. You haven't presented anything in a way that's even remotely attractive." She sounded like a prim, prematurely adult child complaining to her teacher about someone putting a worm down her back.

He felt like an idiot. How had he gotten stuck with this prissy, reedy-voiced thing with a huge forehead who poked and picked over everything that came out of his mouth? He longed for a dim-eyed little slut with a big, bright mouth and black vinyl underwear. What had he had in mind when he brought this girl here, anyway? Her serious, desperate face, panicked and tear-stained. Her ridiculous air of sacrifice and abandonment as he spread-eagled and bound her. White skin that marked easily. Frightened eyes. An exposed personality that could be yanked from her and held out of reach like . . . oh, he could see it only in scraps; his imagination fumbled and lost its grip. He looked at her hatefully self-possessed, compact little form. He pushed her roughly. "Oh, I'd do anything with you," he mimicked. "You would not."

She rolled away on her side, her body curled tightly. He felt her trembling. She sniffed.

"Don't tell me I've broken your heart."

She continued crying.

"This isn't bothering me at all," he said. "In fact, I'm rather enjoying it."

The trembling stopped. She sniffed once, turned on her back and looked at him with puzzled eyes. She blinked. He suddenly felt tired. I shouldn't be doing this, he thought. She is actually a nice person. For a moment he had an impulse to embrace her. He had a stronger impulse to beat her. He looked around the room until he saw a light wood stick that his grandmother had for some reason left standing in the corner. He pointed at it.

"Get me that stick. I want to beat you with it."

"I don't want to."

"Get it. I want to humiliate you even more."

She shook her head, her eyes wide with alarm. She held the blanket up to her chin.

"Come on," he coaxed. "Let me beat you. I'd be much nicer after I beat you."

"I don't think you're capable of being as nice as you'd have to be to interest me at this point."

"All right. I'll get it myself." He got the stick and snatched the blanket from her body.

She sat, her legs curled in a kneeling position. "Don't," she said. "I'm scared."

"You should be scared," he said. "I'm going to torture you." He brandished the stick, which actually felt as though it would break on the second or third blow. They froze in their positions, staring at each other.

She was the first to drop her eyes. She regarded the torn-off blanket meditatively. "You have really disappointed me," she said. "This whole thing has been a complete waste of time."

He sat on the bed, stick in lap. "You don't care about my feelings."

"I think I want to sleep in the next room."

They couldn't sleep separately any better than they could sleep together. She lay curled up on the couch pondering what seemed to be the ugly nature of her life. He lay wound in a blanket, blinking in the dark, as a dislocated, manic and unpleasing revue of his sexual experiences stumbled through his memory in a queasy scramble.

In the morning they agreed that they would return to Manhattan immediately. Despite their mutual ill humor, they fornicated again, mostly because they could more easily ignore each other while doing so.

They packed quickly and silently.

"It's going to be a long drive back," he said. "Try not to make me feel like too much of a prick, okay?"

"I don't care what you feel like."

He would have liked to dump her at the side of the road somewhere, but he wasn't indifferent enough to societal rules to do that. Besides, he felt vaguely sorry that he had made her cry, and while this made him view her grudgingly, he felt obliged not to worsen the situation. Ideally she would disappear, taking her stupid canvas bag with her. In reality, she sat beside him in the car with more solidity and presence than she had displayed since they met on the corner in Manhattan. She seemed fully prepared to sit in silence for the entire six-hour drive. He turned on the radio.

"Would you mind turning that down a little?"

"Anything for you."

She rolled her eyes.

Without much hope, he employed a tactic he used to pacify his wife when they argued. He would give her a choice and let her make it. "Would you like something to eat?" he asked. "You must be starving."

She was. They spent almost an hour driving up and down the available streets trying to find a restaurant she wanted to be in. She finally chose a small, clean egg-and-toast place. Her humor visibly improved as they sat before their breakfast. "I like eggs," she said. "They are so comforting."

He began to talk to her out of sheer curiosity. They talked about music, college, people they knew in common and drugs they used to take as teenagers. She said that when she had taken LSD, she had often lost her sense of identity so completely that she didn't recognize herself in the mirror. This pathetic statement brought back her attractiveness in a terrific rush. She noted the quick dark gleam in his eyes.

"You should've let me beat you," he said. "I wouldn't have hurt you too much."

"That's not the point. The moment was wrong. It wouldn't have meant anything."

"It would've meant something to me." He paused. "But you probably would've spoiled it. You would've started screaming right away and made me stop."

The construction workers at the next table stared at them quizzically. She smiled pleasantly at them and returned her gaze to him. "You don't know that."

He was so relieved at the ease between them that he put his arm around her as they left the restaurant. She stretched up and kissed his neck.

"We just had the wrong idea about each other," she said. "It's nobody's fault that we're incompatible."

"Well, soon we'll be in Manhattan, and it'll be all over. You'll never have to see me again." He hoped she would dispute this, but she didn't.

They continued to talk in the car, about the nature of time, their parents and the injustice of racism.

She was too exhausted to extract much from the pedestrian conversation, but the sound of his voice, the position of his body and his sudden receptivity were intoxicating. Time took on a grainy, dreamy aspect that made impossible conversations and unlikely gestures feasible, like a space capsule that enables its inhabitants to happily walk up the wall. The peculiar little car became a warm, humming cocoon, like a miniature house she had, as a little girl, assembled out of odds and ends for invented characters. She felt as if she were a very young child, when every notion that appeared in her head was new and naked of association and thus needed to be expressed carefully so it didn't become malformed. She wanted to set every one of them before him in a row, as she had once presented crayon drawings to her father in a neat many-colored sequence. Then he would shift his posture slightly or make a gesture that suddenly made him seem so helpless and frail that she longed to protect him and cosset him away, like a delicate pet in a matchbox filled with cotton. She rested her head on his shoulder and lovingly regarded the legs that bent at the knee and tapered to the booted feet resting on the brakes or the accelerator. This was as good as her original fantasy, possibly even better.

"Can I abuse you some more now?" he asked sweetly. "In the car?"

"What do you want to do?"

"Gag you? That's all, I'd just like to gag you."

"But I want to talk to you."

He sighed. "You're really not a masochist, you know."

She shrugged. "Maybe not. It always seemed like I was."

"You might have fantasies, but I don't think you have any concept of a real slave mentality. You have too much ego to be part of another person."

"I don't know, I've never had the chance to try it. I've never met anyone I wanted to do that with."

"If you were a slave, you wouldn't make the choice."

"All right, I'm not a slave. With me it's more a matter of love." She was just barely aware that she was pitching her voice higher and softer than it was naturally, so that she sounded like a cartoon girl. "It's like the highest form of love."

He thought this was really cute. Sure it was nauseating, but it was feminine in a radio-song kind of way.

"You don't seem interested in love. It's not about that for you."

"That's not true. That's not true at all. Why do you think I was so rough back there? Deep down, I'm afraid I'll fall in love with you, that I'll need to be with you and fuck you . . . forever."

He was enjoying himself now. He was beginning to see her as a locked garden that he could sneak into and sit in for days, tearing the heads off the flowers.

On one hand, she was beside herself with bliss. On the other, she was scrutinizing him carefully from behind an opaque facade as he entered her pasteboard scene of flora and fauna. Could he function as a character in this landscape? She imagined sitting across from him in a Japanese restaurant, talking about anything. He would look intently into her eyes. . . .

He saw her apartment and then his. He saw them existing a nice distance apart, each of them blocked off by cleanly cut boundaries. Her apartment bloomed with scenes that spiraled toward him in colorful circular motions and then froze suddenly and clearly in place. She was crawling blindfolded across the floor. She was bound and naked in an S&M bar. She was sitting next to him in a taxi, her skirt pulled up, his fingers in her vagina.

. . . and then they would go back to her apartment. He would beat her and fuck her mouth.

Then he would go home to his wife, and she would make dinner for him. It was so well balanced, the mere contemplation of it gave him pleasure.

The next day he would send her flowers.

He let go of the wheel with one hand and patted her head. She gripped his shirt frantically.

He thought: This could work out fine.

Something Nice

W HAT'S YOUR NAME, sir?" The freckled woman wore green stretch pants, and had her red hair tucked under a neat pink scarf. "Fred?" She was making her naturally coarse voice go soft and moist as warm mayonnaise. "I'd like you to meet my girl-friends, Fred." The four girls stared at him. Two sat up and smiled, holding their purses with tight fingers, their legs pinched together at the knees. A beautiful black-haired girl, with jutting cheekbones and a lush, full mouth, lolled in an orange beanbag chair, her long legs sprawled rudely on the floor, half open and tenting her tight silk dress so you could almost see between her legs. She gawked at him with open disgust.

"Sit up, Jasmine," snapped the stretch-pants woman through her smile. She held out her freckled hands toward the last girl, who sat with one leg tucked underneath her, looking out the window. "And this is Lisette." The girl wore a short red-and-black-checked dress, white ankle socks and black pumps. Her bobbed brown hair was curly. When she turned to face him, her expression was mildly friendly and normal; she could've been looking at anybody or anything.

The strangeness of it all delighted and fascinated him: the falsely gentle voice, the helpless contempt, the choosing of a bored, un-known girl sitting on her ankle, looking out the window.

"Do you see a lady who you'd like to visit with?"

"I'll see Lisette."

The girl stood up and walked toward him as if he were a den-tist, except she was smiling.

The room was pale green. The air in it was bloated with sweat and canned air freshener. There was a bed table set with a plastic container sprouting damp Handi-Wipes, a radio, an ashtray, a Kleenex box and a slimy bottle of oil. The bed was covered by a designer sheet patterned with beige, brown and tan lions lazing happily on the branches of trees or swatting each other. There was an aluminum chair. There was a glass-covered poster for an art exhibit. There was a fish tank with a Day-Glo orange fish castle in it. He lay on the bed naked, waiting for her to join him. He turned on the radio. It was tuned to one of those awful disco stations. *"I specialize in love,"* sang a woman's voice. *"I'll make you feel like new. I specialize in love—let me work on you."*

He smiled as he listened to the music. It evoked the swirling lights of dance floors he'd never been on, the tossing hair and sweat-drenched underwear of girls who danced and drank all night, girls he never saw except in commercials for jeans. He anticipated Lisette as he imagined her, the grip of her blunt-fingered hands, her curly head on his shoulder. Did she dance in places like that, in her white socks and pumps?

She came in with a white sheet under her arm. She clipped across the floor, sharp heels clacking. She turned off the radio. The silence was as disorienting as a sudden roomful of fluorescent light. "I hate that shit," she said. "I hope you don't mind. I have to put this sheet down." She snapped the sheet open and floated it down over him. He scrambled out from under it, banging into the wastebasket as he stepped to the floor.

"Here," he said. He took a corner of the sheet and awkwardly stretched it over the bed.

"No, it's okay, that's good enough." She sat on the bed and stared at him, her small face gone suddenly grave. Her eyes were round and dark. Her muddy black makeup looked as if it had been finger-painted on. He sat down next to her and put his hand on her thigh. She ignored it. He felt as though he was bothering a girl sitting next to him on a bus. His hand sweated on her leg and he took it away. What was wrong? Why wasn't she pulling her dress off over her head, the way they usually did?

"Do you come to places like this often?" she asked.

"Not too much. Every month or so. I'm married, so it's hard to get away."

She looked worried. She reached out with nervous quickness and picked up his hand. "What do people do now, mostly?" she asked.

"What do you mean?"

"I mean I'm new here. You're only my second customer and I don't know what I should do. Well, I know what to *do*, basically, but there's all these little things, like when to take off the dress."

He felt a foolish smile running over his face. Her second customer! "But you've worked before."

"You mean done this before? No, I haven't."

He looked at her, beaming greedily.

"What do you do for a living?" she asked.

"I'm an attorney," he said. "Corporate law." He was lying. He felt cut loose from himself, unmarried, un-old, because of the lie.

"How old are you?"

"How old do you think I am?"

She smiled, and her black eye paint coiled like a snake in the corners of her eyes. "Fifty?"

"You're exactly right." He was fifty-nine. "How about you?"

"Twenty-two."

She looked as though she could be that age, but he had a strong feeling that she was lying too.

"Why do you come to places like this?" She lay across the bed, her head on her hand, her legs folded restfully. "Do you not get along with your wife?"

He leaned against the headboard, his naked legs open. "Oh, I love my wife. It's a very successful marriage. And we have sex, good sex. But it's not everything I want. She's willing to experiment, a little, but she's really not all that interested. It can make you feel foolish to be doing something when you know your partner isn't an equal participant. Besides, this is an adventure for me. Something nice."

"Is it something nice?"

"With you it's going to be very nice."

"How do you know?"

"What a strange question."

She crossed the bed to adjust her body against his, to put her head on his shoulder. She stroked his chest hair. "It's not so strange."

"Well, I just know, that's all."

They kissed. She had a harsh, stubborn kiss.

She took off her checked dress, button by button, very neatly. Her body was extremely pretty: white, curvy and plump. When she took off her high heels he saw that her legs were a little too short and her ankles a bit thick, but he liked them anyway. She folded her dress over the aluminum chair and turned to him with an uptilted chin, looking as if she might break into a trot, like a pony. She was proud of her body.

Her pride was pitiful in the stupid room. It made him feel superior and tender. He gushed a smile and held out his arms. She met him with a surprisingly strong hug, the pouncing grab of a playful animal.

"Goodness, you're healthy."

She grinned and squeezed him. "What do you want to do?"

"We'll play it by ear. Don't be nervous. It's going to be lovely."

The way she touched became unsure. She talked to him as they touched, and her crude, frank words were like pungent flowers against the gray of her shyness. When he touched her hips, he thought he could feel her innermost life on the sensitive surface of her body.

"It was like a honeymoon," he said to her afterward. "Just like I knew it would be."

"Oh, it was not." Her face was in the mirror; she was swiping her mouth with lipstick. "Don't be silly."

"Have you ever been married?"

"Uh-uh."

"Then you don't know what a honeymoon is like." She was right, though. It wasn't like a honeymoon at all.

• • •

She walked him to the door and he kissed her in front of the other girls. The stretch-pants woman smiled. "Good night, Fred," she said.

When he got on the highway to Westchester, he used his push-button device to roll down the windows and drove too fast. When he arrived home he walked through the entire first floor of his house, turning on all the lights. His wife really was out of town, and he didn't like to be alone in a dimly lit house. The refrigerator was clean and neatly stacked with food his wife had prepared for him. He got into his pajamas and slippers and made himself a sandwich of cold cuts and mayonnaise. He stood at the kitchen counter and ate the sandwich from a paper plate with a smiling cat face on it. He thought of Lisette lying across the bed like an arrangement of fruit, her shoulder snuggled against her cheek, watching him clean himself in the bathroom with a cheap pink loofah. She had a curious, sober look on her round face. She's an intelligent girl, he thought. You can see it in her eyes. Why hadn't he told her that he was a veterinarian? He had never lied to a prostitute before. He made himself a piña colada, with lots of crushed ice and a tiny straw—his wife had left a Dixie cup of red-and-white straws next to the blender—and went to bed.

The next night, he drove into Manhattan to see her again.

"Boy, I'm glad to see you tonight," she said as she clacked into the room with the sheet.

"Are you? Why?" He stood to let her crack the sheet above the bed.

"Oh, it's been sort of a bad night. I couldn't stand to deal with another idiot."

"I'm sure you get some pretty undesirable people in here."

"You said it."

"Nobody violent or anything, I hope?"

"No, just stupid." She floated the sheet down and turned to curl against him.

Later, they lay folded together, listening to the sad gurgle of the fish tank. "Look at those poor, dumb things swimming around in there," she said. "They haven't got any idea of the filth going on in here."

"What did you mean about the men who come here? When you said they're . . . just stupid." He'd said "stupid" too loud.

"I don't really mean they're stupid. A lot of them are businessmen. They must have some kind of brain to do that. But they're dumb about women and they're dumb about sex." She rocked him over on his back and lay on him, her fingers perched on his shoulders, her face right against his. "They actually think they can buy you for a hundred and fifty dollars. Like you're going to become sexually excited because they give you money. I mean they can pay you to do certain things. But they can't buy anyone for a hundred and fifty dollars." She rolled off him and flopped on her back. "It's so retarded. They don't have any idea of what good sex is, so they wouldn't know you can't buy it." She turned her head to him. "I hope I'm not insulting you. I'm not talking about you."

He stuck his body up on one elbow so he could look at her. "No. No, I think it's very interesting. I'm flattered that you choose to tell me these things." Her stomach was sticking out like a little bread loaf. He tickled it lightly.

She scratched her stomach. "Why did you come back so soon?"

"Don't you remember last night? I find our, uh, sex highly erotic. Not because I pay for it, but because it just is." He paused to let her react. She stared at him and blinked. "Besides, I like you. I think there's something between us. I think that if I were a few years younger and we met under slightly different circumstances, we might even have what's now called a relationship."

She smiled and looked at the happy lions snoozing on the designer sheets. He put his hand on hers. "The first night I came here, you were uncertain, kind of shy. You came out and admitted it, you asked me questions. You trusted me. Tonight when you were mad, you didn't put on a phony smile. You let off steam, told me how you felt. You didn't treat me like a customer. That's nice. There's hardly anybody that'll be real with you like that anymore. Sometimes even my wife isn't honest with me."

She looked up from the smiling lions. "You shouldn't come to prostitutes looking for honesty."

"You're not a prostitute. Don't say that about yourself."

"What do you think I am?"

"You just happen to be a pretty, sexy girl who, uh—"

"I have sex for money."

"Well, all right." He slapped her thigh nervously. "You're right. You're a prostitute." It sounded so horrible. "But you're still a wonderful girl." He grabbed her and snuggled her.

"You don't know me."

"You're wonderful." He squeezed her like he wanted to break her ribs. She shoved her pelvis against him, threw her arms and one leg around him and squeezed with all her slippery might. She smiled with half-closed eyes, and bit her grinning lip. He squeezed harder. She jammed her elbows into his sides and he made a meek "whoof" noise.

He dropped his arms, panting. "God, you're strong. How did such a small person get so strong?"

She grinned like a wolf. "I dunno." She let go and rolled off, and padded into the bathroom.

He followed her. "Are you a gymnast? A dancer?"

"No. I used to work out with weights in school." She dabbed between her legs with a nubbly white washcloth.

"University?"

"Yeah." She grabbed a fat economy-size jar of mentholated mouthwash, threw her head back and dumped a big splash into her mouth. Her cheeks worked vigorously as she sloshed it to and fro.

"Do you show your strength in the way you deal with people? I mean, outside of this place?"

She spat a green burst of mouthwash into the sink and looked at him. "Yeah. I do."

"How do you make them aware of it?"

She leaned against the sink, facing him with her arms behind her, her face thoughtful and soft. "I just . . . don't let people sway my thinking. I don't mold myself to fit what other people think I am." She came forward and put her arms around him. "It's interesting that you find strength in women attractive."

"Why?"

"Don't most older men like passive, dependent women?"

"Oh, that's an awful stereotype. Don't believe it."

"Is your wife a strong woman?"

"Yes, she is."

"Is she a lawyer too?"

"No. She's an antiquarian. She's got a small rare-book business."

"Did you meet her in college?"

"Yes. She studied art history and Latin. I was very impressed by that."

"Was she the first person you had sex with?"

"Almost."

"I bet that's why you see prostitutes." She let go of him and hurried to get dressed. The outermost flesh of her backside jiggled as she balanced on one spike heel and stuck the other through a leg of her underpants.

"What do you mean?"

"You had so little chance to screw around when you were young. You're trying to get it now." Her fingers were flying over the tiny buttons of her checked dress.

"You know, I think you're writing a book. That's what you're doing here. You're one of those journalists doing undercover work on prostitution."

She smiled miserably. "No."

"What do you do, besides work here? I think you do something. Am I right?"

"Of course I do something." She said "do" very sarcastically. She trotted to the mirror and got out her shiny silver lipstick case.

"What? What do you do?" He came toward her.

"I don't like to talk about it here." She opened her black leather bag to replace the lipstick. He glimpsed a roll of money and a packet of condoms in sky-blue tinfoil.

"Why don't you like to talk about it?"

"It makes me unhappy."

The telephone by the bed rasped, indicating the end of their hour.

He saw her again the following night, and the night after that. He relished the way she laughed and playfully squeezed him around the stomach with her hefty thighs, or impatiently squiggled out from under him so they could change position. Her nonchalant reaction to his efforts to impress her sexually made him believe that her excitement, when it did occur, was real, that she wanted him. But if he so much as put a hand where she didn't want it, she'd fiercely slap it away and snap, "I don't like that."

"That's why I like you so much," he said. "You don't let me get away with anything. You're straightforward. Like my wife."

During that time, she told him that her real name was Jane. She still wouldn't talk to him about her life outside the pale green room. Instead, she asked him questions about himself. He was too embarrassed by now to tell her that he'd lied about his job. The lie turned out to be a mistake. Not only was she unimpressed by his false attorneyhood, she was an animal lover. The longest conversation they ever had on a single subject was about a cat that she'd had for fifteen years, until the fat, asthmatic thing finally keeled over. "He had all black fur except for his paws and his throat patch. He looked like he was wearing a tuxedo with a white cravat and gloves, and he was more of a gentleman than any human being I've ever known. I saw him protect a female cat from a dog once."

The cute stories he could've told about all the kittens and puppies that came into his office, clinging to the shirts of their owners, the birds with broken wings in white-spattered boxes!

The fifth night he came to see her, she wasn't sitting in the waiting room with the other girls. "Where's Jane?" he asked the stretch-pants woman nervously.

"Jane? You must mean *Lisette*. She's busy right now," she answered in her placid, salad-oily voice. "Would you like to see another lady?"

A very young girl with burgundy hair smiled brightly at him. She was clutching a red patent-leather purse in purple-nailed hands.

"I'll wait for Lisette."

The stretch-pants woman widened her naked-lashed eyes in approval. "All right, Fred, just sit down and make yourself comfortable. Would you like something to drink?"

She brought him a horribly flat, watered-down Scotch in a plastic cup. He held it, smiling and sweating.

The burgundy-headed girl curled her legs up on the couch and turned back to her Monopoly game with the contemptuous black-haired girl, who lay across the couch like an eel on a market stand. The stretch-pants woman tried to talk to him.

"Do you work around here, Fred?"

"No."

"What kind of business are you in?"

"Nothing. I mean, I'm retired." The patches of shirt under his arms were glued with sweaty hair-lace. Jane was being mauled by a fat oaf who didn't care that you could feel her innermost life on her skin.

The stretch-pants woman asked him to step into the kitchen. This house advertised its discretion and made sure men did not meet each other. He saw only the man's dismal black-suited shape through the slats of the swinging kitchen door as he stood there holding his drink, the ice cubes melting into a depressing fizz. He heard the black shape's blurred rumble and Jane's indifferent voice. She sounded much nicer when she said good-bye to him. The pale-eyed hostess opened the swinging door and gave him a flat smile. "Okay, sir, would you like to step out?"

Jane stood smiling in her checked dress, her hands behind her back, one white-socked ankle crossing the other, her chin tilted up. He remembered how he had seen her first, how she could've been any girl, any bland, half-friendly face behind any counter. He felt a funny-bone twinge as he realized how her body, her voice, her every fussy gesture had become part of a Jane network, a world of smells, sounds and touches that found its most acute focus when she had her legs around his back.

• • •

The minute she came into the room, he went to her and put his arms around her hips. "Hello, Jane."

"Hi."

"It was strange not seeing you out there waiting for me."

She looked puzzled.

"I guess I somehow got used to thinking of you as my own little girl. I didn't like the idea that you were with some other guy. Silly, huh?"

"Yes." She broke away and snapped the sheet out over the bed. "Do you say things like that because you think I like to hear them?"

"Maybe. Some of the girls do, you know."

He could feel the sarcasm of her silence.

He watched her pull her dress off over her head and drop it on the aluminum chair. "I guess it's only natural that you've begun to get jaded."

She snorted. "I wouldn't call it that."

"What would you call it?"

She didn't answer. She sat on the bed and bent to take off her heels, leaving her socks on. When she looked at him again she said, "Do you really think it's a good idea for you to come to see me every night? It's awfully expensive. I know lawyers make a lot of money, but still. Won't your wife wonder where it's going?"

He sat next to her and put his hand on her shoulder. "Don't you see how special you are? No other girl I've seen like this would ever have thought to say something like that. All they can think of is how to get more money out of me and here you are worrying about how much I'm spending. I'm not trying to flatter you, you *are* different."

"Aren't you worried about getting AIDS?"

"From a girl like you? C'mon, don't put yourself down."

She smiled, sad and strained, but sort of affectionate, and put her hands on his shoulders. She felt to him like one of his puppy patients embracing him as he carried it across the room for a shot.

"I'm sorry I'm being so shitty," she said. "I just hate this job and this place."

"Here," he said. "I'm going to buy two hours, so we can just relax and unwind. You just lie down and get snuggled up in the sheet." He got up and turned off the light. He found a romantic jazz station on the radio. He undressed and got under the sheet with her, wrapping them both in a ball. He held her neck and felt her forehead against his shoulder. Her limbs were nestled and docile, as if all her stiff, pony-trot energy had vanished. The dim light of the gurgling fish tank cast an orangy glow over the room. "This is so nice and glamorous," he said.

"When is your wife coming back?" asked a voice from the nuzzling bundle on his arm.

"In three days." He sighed and stared at the stupid, lovely slivers of fish darting around their ugly castle.

Of course he knew that concern for his financial situation wasn't the only reason she'd suggested that he shouldn't see her so often. She was probably sick of him. He remembered dating well enough to know that women didn't like to be pursued too closely. It could seem sappy, he supposed, to come grinning in there after her every single night. The next night he would stay home, and read or watch television.

He enjoyed making dinner for himself. There were still a lot of good things left in the refrigerator — herring, a chunk of potato salad that was only slightly rancid, cream cheese, a jar of artichoke hearts, egg bread. It was too messy to eat in the kitchen — the counter was covered with encrusted plates and pans filled with silverware and water.

He arranged the slices and oily slabs on two different plates and carried the stuff into the living room to put on the coffee table. He clicked on the TV with his remote-control device, flicked the channels around a few times and then ignored it. He ate with his fingers and a plastic fork, mentally feeling over the events of the day, like a blind person groping through a drawer of personal effects. There had been the usual parade of cats and dogs, and one exotic bird with a mysterious illness. He had no idea what to do with the crested, vividly plumed thing, which was apparently worth a lot of money. He had pretended that he did, though, and the bird was sitting in his kennel now, gaping fiercely at the cats with its hooked beak.

Then there was the dog that he had had to put to sleep, a toothless, blind, smelly old monster with toenails like a dinosaur's. He thought the dog was probably grateful for the injection, and he said so, but that didn't console the homely adolescent girl who insisted on holding it right up until the end, tears running from under her glasses and down her pink, porous face. Poor lonely girl, he thought. He had wanted to say, "Don't worry, dear, you're going to grow up to be a beauty. You're going to get married and have lots of wonderful children." Except it probably wasn't true.

He picked up his remote-control device and switched channels thoughtfully. What would Jane think when he didn't show up? Would she think he'd gotten bored with her, that he was never coming back? Would she go home wondering what had happened? He tried to picture her in her apartment. She had told him it was very small, only one room with a tiny bathroom. She said the bathroom had big windows and a skylight, and that she had so many plants in there that you couldn't use the toilet without arranging yourself around the plants. She said she didn't have a chair or a couch, that she sat on the floor to eat. When she came home from work she often ordered Chinese food and ate it straight from the cardboard boxes set out on the floor between her spread legs.

"What do you have for breakfast?" he asked.

"Ice cream, sometimes. If it's warm."

"What do you find to do in that little room?"

"I read a lot."

"What do you like to read?"

She named a few writers, one that he'd been forced to read in college and others he'd never heard of.

He picked up a tiny bit of herring and mashed it with the edges of his front teeth. Maybe he could start seeing Jane in her apartment. It would be more money for her certainly. He would like to spend time in that funny little place. He could buy her a chair. Maybe even a table.

He wouldn't be able to see Jane much at all once Sylvia got back. He thought of his wife getting on the plane in her green-and-white dress, the handle of her wicker suitcase in hand, her gray hair wound into an elegant bun that displayed her graceful neck and gently erect shoulders. Her smile was beautiful when she turned to wave good-bye.

He pictured Sylvia sitting in her favorite armchair across from him. She would be relaxed but sitting up straight on the tautly stuffed, salmon-colored cushions. Her legs would be crossed at the ankle. She would have her pale beige glasses on her nose, she would be in a trance over her latest book catalogues. If he stood up and put his hand on her shoulder, he would feel how slender and strong she still was, how well defined her small bones were.

He thought of her collection of rare books, arranged and locked in the glass cabinet in a sunny corner of her study. They were beautiful to look at and extremely expensive; other book dealers had offered her thousands of dollars for some of them. Every time he looked at them, he felt depressed.

One Christmas, he bought Sylvia a book entitled *Beautiful Sex*. It made him unhappy to remember that night when, with *Beautiful Sex* lying open on their bed to reveal a series of glossy pink-and-white photos, she cooperatively arranged herself into one of the more conventional positions illustrated, sighing as she did so. "Now, honey," she said, "tell the truth. Don't you feel foolish doing this?"

He clicked off the TV and left the room, making a mental note to put the plates in the dishwasher before he went to bed.

The next day he drove to Manhattan right after work, without stopping at home for a shower. Perhaps Jane would notice the vague animal smell on him. She might ask him about it and he could tell her the truth about what he did.

It was already dark when he reached the city. He drove slowly through Times Square, fascinated by the night's ugliness. He stopped for a red light and looked up at a movie marquee towering on the corner, its dead white face advertising *The Spanking of Cindy.* There was a short man in a black leather jacket standing by the box office, hunching his cadaverous shoulders in the wind. "Now there's a queer," thought Fred. "Wonder what he's doing in front of that movie house?" He looked at the marquee again, and noticed that the billboard next to it was painted with a girl in jeans thrusting her bottom out, her blond hair swirling across her back, her mouth open in laughter. It was an ad for jeans, but it suited the movie; he vaguely wondered if it had been arranged that way. He turned his head to look at the other side of the street and saw a broken old woman lying unconscious in the middle of the sidewalk with her face against the concrete, her ragged dress spattered across her ugly thighs. He was disgusted to see a young man pissing against the wall not two feet away from her. People were stepping over her as if she were an object, vicious people, it seemed to him, swinging their arms and legs in every direction, working their mouths, yelling at each other, eating hot dogs or Italian ices. What would it be like to be among them? He watched a couple of hookers in miniskirts and leather boots kick their way through a pile of garbage, screaming with laughter.

As soon as he got to a different neighborhood, he stopped at a Chinese flower store and bought Jane a single long-stemmed rose.

"Just so you wouldn't think I'd forgotten you," he said when he handed it to her.

"Thanks." She laid it on the night table, between the bottle of baby oil and the flowered Kleenex box. "Were you sick?"

"No. I just had some . . . things to do. Did you miss me?"

"Yeah." She began undoing her buttons.

"Listen, Jane. Tomorrow night will be the last night I can see you for a while. I was thinking maybe we could do something special."

"Like what?"

"Like you could call in sick and we could meet somewhere for dinner."

She put her hands in her lap and stared at him with something like alarm in her wide, smudged eyes.

"We could have dinner, go to a movie or a concert—whatever you'd like. Then we could go to a hotel—or maybe your apartment—and spend the night together."

She looked at her nails and picked them.

"Of course I realize that I can't ask you to take a night off work without making it worth your while. You'd do all right."

"How much?"

"Five hundred."

She didn't say anything.

"It could be very nice. We'd have time to really act like people in a relationship. What do you say?"

"I don't know."

"What are your reservations?"

"I don't think people in these circumstances can act like people having a relationship."

"Well, maybe you're right about that. But still it might be fun. I'd love to talk to you about a movie we'd seen or . . ."

"I think you'd be surprised if you found out what I'm like outside of here."

"I can't believe I wouldn't like you."

"You'd think I was weird."

"I'm not as closed-minded as you think."

"It's just that we might not have anything to talk about."

She didn't notice the animal smell.

He waited for half an hour at their appointed meeting place. He wasn't surprised when she stood him up. He was somewhat surprised when he called the escort service to make an appointment and they told him she'd quit. She'd often told him she hated it and that she was going to quit soon, but girls talked like that all the time and stayed for months, even years.

Sylvia returned the next day, smiling and suntanned, happy to wash the dishes on the kitchen counter and pick up the damp, scrunched-up towels that were wadded up on every rack in the bathroom. She told him nice stories about the Arizona desert and the book fair she'd gone to there. He made love to her in a quiet, respectful way. She put her slender arms around his shoulders and held him tight. But when he tried to show her some of the things he'd done with Jane, he could feel her body become docile and patient.

He drove into Manhattan about once a month to pay for girls. He went to different establishments each time, hoping to find Jane. Every time he saw a new girl he suffered from nostalgia and the irritating nag of unfavorable comparison.

When he thought of her he didn't feel love or anything like it. He felt a sort of painful fondness. He remembered having a similar feeling when he ran into a girl he'd been crazy about in college and saw that she'd gotten fat and was buying a box of Pampers. It was strange to be having that feeling now for someone he met in a brothel.

It was almost a year later when he went into Manhattan one afternoon to do Christmas shopping. The city had a different quality during the day. When he thought of daytime Manhattan, the first thing he imagined was a pretty young woman with dark, wavy hair and an unnatural burst of red on both cheeks, walking down the wide, crowded sidewalks more quickly and sharply than anyone had to, her worn, brightly colored shoes marching in close, narrow steps, her cheap, fashionable jacket open to show her belted waist, her handbag held tightly under her arm, her head turned away from anyone who might look at her, turned so she could skim the window displays as she clipped by, one hand jammed into a pocket of her jacket, nothing swinging loose. And then he thought of a lumbering, middle-aged man in a suit, his glasses on the tip of his nose, a lace of greasy crumbs on his lapels, his briefcase clutched at his side, rolling down the street as fast as his plump body would go, jacket flapping open, his bored eyes skimming quickly over the girl and every other girl like her as he rushed to the office.

There was something sad and poignant about this image, but that didn't prevent him from spending as much time staring at girls as he spent shopping. At the end of the day he'd found only two gifts—a sweater-guard made of twin silver bunnies for a teenaged niece and, for Sylvia, an elegant old-fashioned wristwatch from a Village watch shop.

By the time he had found these gifts it was late afternoon and he was hungry. The watch shop was close to a particular café he liked because the food was good and because he enjoyed looking at the strangely dressed young people who often went there.

The hostess, a tall girl with a high, perspiring forehead and pleasantly freckled cheeks, smiled as she ran toward him with a long plastic menu, and immediately raced him to a corner table that had yellow flowers in a green bottle on it. "Enjoy," she panted, and ran off. He shook off his heavy coat and looked over the crowd with relish. He picked up the menu and glanced at the table on his left. From then on the rest of the people in the room became a herd of anonymous colored shapes that could've been eating their fingers for all he cared. Jane was sitting next to him. She was with a boy. She glanced at him too quickly for him to see her expression. She immediately put her elbow on the table and her hand to her face.

He looked away. He squeezed the laminated menu between his fingers. He read the description of cold pasta three times. He turned his head and stared at her. She'd grown her hair out and was wearing it up in a ponytail that looked like a ball of brown wool. Even with her hand blocking her face, he could see that she wore almost no makeup, that her skin looked fresh and rosy in daylight. She was wearing an old cream-colored sweater with pink and blue tulips woven into it.

He stared at the boy who sat across the table from her. He was a homely kid in his early twenties with a thick thatch of badly cut sandy hair that roared up over his forehead in a hideous bush. His crooked tortoiseshell glasses had one arm held on by a piece of grayish masking tape, and he wore a brown sweater thick enough to be a coat. His complexion was ruddy and coarse, his expression horribly cheerful.

On a cruel impulse, he leaned forward and leered at the kid.

The boy glanced at him affably and buried his spoon in the bowl of stew he had before him.

"Yeah," he said. "Simone's been experiencing a lot of rejection from her old friends."

"I'm not really rejecting her," said Jane. "I just want to put some distance between us emotionally. Enough so that she doesn't feel compelled to call me every time her psychotic girlfriend starts slapping her around."

She was going to sit there and continue her conversation.

"How many times has it been now?" asked the ugly kid through a mouthful of stew.

"Five, counting the last girlfriend, three times at six in the morning. I mean, my God, where does she find these women? I didn't think lesbians were into beating each other up."

A waitress in a short black leather skirt and leopard-skin tights charged his table. "Are you ready to order?"

"No, no, not yet." She smiled and roared off. He lowered his head to the plastic menu. He was not sure why this experience was such an unpleasant one.

"I mean, her life is her life," said Jane. "But the last time she called she actually got me over there to mediate between her and this crazed, muscle-bound black belt in God knows what, and they're screaming at each other and Simone is threatening to cut her wrist, and oh, it was a mess."

"It sounds very theatrical."

"It's like not only is she going to be a masochistic asshole, she wants an audience. I know I'm being cruel."

"I don't think you're cruel. Most people wouldn't have put up with it as long as you did."

"It's so tragic, though. She's such a great person. And I know at least two really attractive, charming girls who're dying to get into her pants, but she's not interested. She likes bitches."

"Look, Simone sets herself up for disaster. She always has. Then she tries to drag anyone within range into it."

They gnawed their food righteously. Jane still had her elbow up and her hand blocking her face.

"How's the job search going?" she asked.

"It looks good so far. Like I said, I think I did all right at Ardis films. And I know somebody who used to work there. The only thing about that place is that the people are so pretentious. Everybody there is a 'close personal friend' of Herzog or Beth B. or somebody. Everybody has this certain pompous accent, especially when they say 'film.'"

"That's professional New York," said Jane. "People who work in the arts are always that way."

"Maybe I'll just come work in the museum with you."

"If we're not on strike. And it looks like we're going to be."

"Could you survive on free-lance work if that happened?"

"Maybe." She dropped the hand at her chin, exposing her face to him. "I don't know."

He got up from the table, looking straight ahead, and slowly gathered his coat around his shoulders. He could sense no movement of her head turning to look at him as he left the restaurant. He wouldn't realize that he'd left the bag containing the bunny sweater-guard and Sylvia's watch under the table until he arrived home in Westchester.

An Affair, Edited

WHEN HE SAW her on the way to work in the morning, he ignored her, even though he hadn't seen her for four years. They had met at the University of Michigan. It had been such a brief, disturbing affair that he didn't even think of her as an old girlfriend. His memory of her was like a filmy scrap of dream discovered on the floor during the drowsy journey from bed to toilet, or a girl in an advertisement that catches in the cluttered net of memory and persists, waiting to commit sex acts with you later that night. Her slight body and pale movements intensified his impression. He had his Walkman on when they passed each other, and his blotted hearing made it easier for him to ignore her. She approached, her face tilted toward him, quizzical and apprehensive. She passed him and vanished, replaced by a girl in a suit and two staring, striding men with briefcases. She did not seem to notice that he ignored her; in fact she might have ignored him too. Their affair had ended badly.

He descended into the dank grayness of the subway, relishing slightly her surprise appearance. He had never gone to work this way before. It was probably the route she always took.

He wondered what kind of job she had; she had been wearing blue jeans stuffed into short, scuffed black boots and a tweed coat with a purple scarf folded around her neck. He wondered if it had embarrassed her to encounter him in a suit, obviously the holder of the better job. In college they had often discussed how one should deal with the world in order to become successful. He saw her ghost lying on its side on his rumpled sheets, resting on one elbow, her then-long hair lying randomly on her shoulders, telling him what she thought about success. He smiled a little. The subway banged harshly into view, and he pressed forward with the sleepy, odorous mass he joined each morning.

He emerged in a cleaner area of Manhattan and entered the spinning glass doors of a gray building that was as grainy and oblong as a cartoon drawing of an office building in *The New Yorker*. He worked for an independent film distribution company that dealt mainly in foreign films. It was a prestigious place to work, and he was proud of himself for getting the job right after graduation. When he first started there, it had thrilled him to know that he could attend screenings of important films, take his friends to see them free, and meet famous people every now and then.

The office was small and contained mixed knotty-legged furniture and the square orange desks of secretaries and assistants. There was a bulletin board tacked with magazine headings and photographs slabbed together. "Hi, Joel," said the receptionist. She was echoed by two other assistants as he walked by. He stopped to chat with Cecilia, a colleague with whom he had had an affair during his first two years at the company. Now that it was over, they were friends and often had lunch. She talked to him about her date the night before.

"I'm intrigued," she said. "He's done work for"—she named two fashionable directors—"and next summer, he's going to France to work with Eric Rohmer. He's very good-looking. And funny and intelligent. Everything."

"Sounds perfect. Where did Mr. Wonderful take you?"

"The Gloucester House. That seafood place around Fiftieth?"

"And then what?"

She returned his playful leer and told him.

He didn't feel belittled by Cecilia's wealthier, more prestigious boyfriends, partly, he supposed, because he felt that he had somehow joined their ranks sheerly by virtue of his affair with her. He did feel slightly humiliated by Cecilia's speedy rise in the company, however, which had left him behind in the same job he'd been doing for three years. "My inner time clock isn't the same as everyone else's." It occurred to him that he'd said that a long time ago to the phantom girl he'd seen on the street.

He sat at his desk, looked through yesterday's mail and then, bracing himself, he got on the phone. He spent a great deal of time calling student film groups and guilds across the country, trying to interest them in Ariel films. He had always been very good at it, but now he had to fend off the idea that it might be depressing. One of the women he currently went out to dinner with also did most of her work on the phone. She had once said to him, in her nervously irritated way, that doing most of her business by phone had begun to seem strange to her. "Think about it," she said, gripping her noodle-bearing fork in tight, elegant fingers. "All day long you're in that room by yourself, talking to disembodied voices. Hundreds of 'em during the year. You're immersed in floating utterances. You don't know these people, you don't even know what they look like. There's no handshake, nothing. Just a pattern of sounds coming out of a plastic thing with holes."

"You're exaggerating," he said. "For comic effect."

"Barely. I never should've taken this job. I've always hated talking on the phone."

Why was he always attracted to these small, dramatic women?

He got on the phone and began selling Ariel's latest release — an American film he disliked and didn't want to distribute. The plot was ridiculous; he was surprised when it was met with such a friendly critical response. It concerned a young Chinese woman working in a Japanese geisha bar in San Francisco, who is trying to find a relative she has never seen, an uncle who disappeared shortly after a murder that took place during a meeting of an obscure, crackpot Chinese political group. The woman never finds her uncle, although someone keeps leaving photos of him in her path, along with impossible excerpts from the *I Ching*. It was idiotic, but popular with college students. "It's not a political film per se, although there is a political element present. It's more about communal identity and illusion," he said to buyers.

After lunch there was a meeting about several new films under consideration. One of them was based on a novella by a famous South American writer about a child forced into prostitution by her grandmother. Listening to the discussion of the film reminded him again of the girl he had passed on the street that morning. The subject of child prostitution almost always did, even after all this time. This was because she had told him, almost on meeting him, that she had left home at the age of fifteen and had, when she was sixteen, become a hooker for two months. She was a twenty-two-year-old college junior when they met, but the information had formed a fascinating gauze that floated over her for the entire time that he knew her.

He went to a screening of the South American film after work. It was a beautifully photographed political allegory, the kind he nearly always liked. But the frame that stayed with him had nothing to do with politics. The dark child, raped by her brutal first customer, turns her head to avoid his kiss, and a flat, brilliant fish swimming in imaginary water is superimposed, with rippling subtlety, over her face, a memory, perhaps, of the pretty fish tank in her grandmother's demolished mansion.

When he got home he called one of the women he dated. "Nothing special," he said. "Just checking up on you. Seeing how you are."

She was pleased by his call, and told him she'd been depressed all week because of an agent's reaction to her writing. He lost interest in the conversation sooner than he'd expected. He told her he had to go, but that he'd call her soon. Then he called the woman who hated telephones. She was depressed too. Her father had been calling to talk to her about how awful his life was, sometimes before she made it out of the apartment in the morning. That was a little more entertaining, but he cut that short too.

He made himself a quick dinner of packaged vegetable-flavored Indian noodles with butter. Then he opened a can of sardines and took them into his bedroom to eat in front of the TV. The best thing that he found to watch was a talk show featuring a beautiful teenaged movie star who had recently performed an erotic nude scene in a box office hit. He liked to watch her. Her precise, careful manner would have seemed stiff in a grown woman, but was charming in a child sex star. Half-formed illusions about meeting and seducing her absorbed him as he ate his noodles.

He went to bed early. When he woke up, he realized that he'd been dreaming. A fourteen-year-old girl had been given to him to take care of by some vague authority. She was a lovely tall child with wide solemn eyes and long dark hair. She hated clothes and walked around the apartment naked. He was not just excited by this, he was exhilarated and moved by her innocence. He remembered an image of her bicycling down the block in unconcerned leggy nakedness, her hair catching the sunlight. The dream then took an unfortunate turn. She was chased by a host of anxious neighbors, all trying to drape her with garments. They caught her and wrested her from his care with accusations of indecency and child molestation.

The dream left him with a sense of irrational discouragement and a mosquito-bite feeling of loss. He moped as he brushed his teeth. He wished his roommate would come back from Italy. He had never been to Europe or anywhere else, and was sick of people going.

He walked the unusual route again. Again he saw her, in almost exactly the same place. This time she looked directly at him and even showed a slight smile on her face. She nodded shyly at him. Not meeting her look, he half nodded and she was gone. Her severely bobbed hair was pretty, but not as pretty as her long hair had been.

He had lunch with Cecilia that afternoon. They ate their corned beef on rye and cream cheese with lox in a diner peopled by waiters who looked like they'd met with utter disappointment and became attached to it. Cecilia was reassuring. She was not small or theatrical. Her shoulder-length hair was blond, her plump body calm. She had a long way of saying her words, a relaxed but vaguely predatory way of turning her head. She came from a wealthy family, and he supposed that was where she got her assurance. Her background was part of what made her attractive to him. He wasn't after her money (although he wouldn't mind, certainly, if one day she spoke to her parents about financing a film project of his own); there was simply something foreign and delightful about this rich girl who had been safely surrounded by money all her life. The perfume of wealth graced her casually, like grass stains on the skin of a lazy child sleeping in a garden. He pictured her as an adolescent, lounging on her huge unmade, canopied and silk-sheeted bed. She was in her underwear, she was reading Tolstoy, occasionally scratching herself and eating from a box of chocolates, although he knew that Cecilia didn't like candy and never had.

"It's so interesting," she said. "Now that I'm closer to success, I've become much less interested in it. I've always known that I would be successful, that I just had to work for it. But it was always out of reach, so I obsessed about it all the time. It was a goal. Now it's more like a natural outcome, another element of my life to be experienced. It's not even important anymore. There are so many other things in life. It's silly to be so narrow."

"That's easy for you to say," he said. "Things are always less important once you're assured of having them."

"It's not that it isn't important, it's just that I'm not focusing on it to the exclusion of everything else. But I'm sure I'll enjoy it when it happens. If anything, it's more real to me now, not like something I'm going to acquire."

He chewed without answering, and she flicked the corners of her mouth with her tongue.

"I think I'm going to Italy in a few months," she said. "I'm really excited about it. I want to meet an Italian film producer and have an affair with him."

"My roommate is in Italy," he said.

"You told me."

In a few months he would say, "My friend Cecilia is in Italy." He looked at her serene face, her resting throat, her slightly upturned chin. He had slept with her for almost two years. She had sucked him off with that mouth. He thought: My friend, Cecilia. My friend.

When he returned to his office he got on the WATS line and called Wilson. Wilson had been a close friend while they were in Ann Arbor. Now he was stuck teaching undergraduates in a geology department in Washington, D.C. Joel called him about twice a month to gossip about other people they'd gone to school with. He knew Wilson kept in touch with the woman he'd seen again this morning.

"Do you know what Sara's doing? Do you know where she's working?"

There was a breath of silence before Wilson answered. "She's all right. I think she's still working in a bar in the East Village."

"Has she gotten anywhere with her painting?"

"I don't think so. Not since the little show she was in at that club. Why?"

"I've seen her twice on the street this week. We haven't had a chance to talk. I just wondered what she was up to."

Wilson had disapproved of Joel's relationship with Sara, even though he'd been morbidly fascinated by it. Even though it had raised Joel in his esteem.

Joel got off the phone and gazed at the morose buildings standing in a clump outside his window.

Interrupted, static-ridden commercials for memories of Sara flitted mutely through his mind, chopped up and poorly edited — Sara before he knew her, a small slender person walking down State Street with her books, wearing jeans and fawn-colored boots. She had a very stiff walk despite her round hips, a tight sad mouth and wide abstracted eyes. She was always alone whenever he saw her, and always appeared vaguely surprised by everything around her. He saw her propped up in his bed, reading a book about South Africa. He saw her sitting across a table, a sauce-red shrimp in her fingers, chatting about her experience as a hooker, oblivious to stares from the next table. She appeared seated in the dark of the film auditorium, her hand at her jaw, her booted legs tossed over the next few chairs, her tongue snapping sarcastically.

"It's so dishonest, it's so middle-class. Who does he think he's shocking? It's such a reaction to convention. It's babyish."

"You don't understand the concept of subversion," he said.

"I know more about subversion than anybody else in this stupid town," she said.

The clips sped up and blurred into glimpses. Her melancholic paleness in the dark, the sheets rumpled to reveal her gray-tinged mattress. The stark lumpiness of her spine and shoulder blades as she reached across him to snatch a "snot rag" from its box. The dry toughness of her heels. The nervous stickiness of her fingers. "Hurt me," she said. "Hurt me."

He could feel his eyes become clouded with privacy as he slipped discreetly into a sheltering cave of sexual fantasy. His focus wobbled, he slipped out again. In Ann Arbor he had pierced his ear, he had worn a beret sometimes. He had written articles in the student paper on labor unions. He had brought Andy Warhol to Cinema I. He saw himself drunk on the curb outside the Del Rio, talking with Wilson and vomiting. They were talking about politics and sex, Wilson mainly talking politics, since he rarely fucked anybody. Joel had just met Sara. "She's great. She's every man's dream. I can't tell you how, because she made me promise not to." He turned and barfed.

Everything was so important in Ann Arbor, so fraught with the tension held tight in the bud of fantasy before it bursts into gaily striped attempt. "I have this fantasy of becoming an anarchist on the Left Bank," he said to Sara. "Throwing bombs and creating a disturbance."

"I want to become a good painter," she said. "Or a great painter."

"Listen," he said, raising himself above her on his elbow. "I want you to be strong. You've come so far in spite of everything. I want you to be successful."

"I am strong," she said. Her eyes were serene. "I'm stronger than anyone else I know."

He cleared his eyes and looked once more at the querulous buildings sweating in the afternoon heat. Of course, she hadn't been strong at all. He remembered the tremulous whine coming out of the phone during their last conversation. "I'm scared," she'd wept. "I feel like I don't exist, I can't eat, I can't do anything. I want to kill myself."

"Look, I grew up in a normal, happy family," he'd said. "I'm well adjusted. I can't identify with this self-esteem crisis, or whatever it is you've got. Anyway, we've only known each other for a few months and I'm not obligated to listen to your problems. You should call a psychiatrist, and anyway I have to take a bath right now."

He couldn't stand weak women.

He went to a nightclub in the evening with his friend Jerry and two of Jerry's hulking lawyer friends. They went to a club that made them and a lump of other people line up outside the door for inspection by a haughty doorman who might or might not admit them, depending on whether or not he liked their appearance. Joel and Jerry, with the lawyers, had to wait an inordinate length of time while a series of habitual clubbers insouciantly gained entrance. It could've been humiliating, but instead it was an intriguing form of entertainment, a piece of behavior to be observed. One of the lawyers kept saying, "I don't want to go in there anyway. This is a drag. Let's go somewhere else."

"No, it's really good in here," said Jerry. "You'll see."

They eventually gained admission and roamed the three floors of the club, greedily looking around. Joel drank one paper cup of watered-down alcohol after another and stared at the moiling sweat-dampened crowd with an attitude of wistful contempt. They were coiffed like Dr. Seuss characters and dressed like children in their parents' clothes. At one time he had wanted to be like them. Now he thought they were stupid, although he still liked to look at them. He saw a girl standing alone at a bar, dressed like a twelve-year-old's idea of a hooker. Tight black bodice, short flared ballerina skirt. She was small, she stood with her ankles together. He edged along the wall, pretending to study the material hung up as art. He remembered the blow-up doll he had once hung up in his Ann Arbor apartment as a party decoration. It wore Sara's clothes and bore, with Scotch tape, a sign that read "Hurt Me Beat Me Fuck Me." Wilson had said, "Joel, come on. This is too much. It's not funny." Joel continued toward the girl at the bar, fighting the anxious crimp in his shoulders.

The terse conversation with her didn't result in her phone number on a piece of paper in his pocket. He found the lawyers again and stalked around with them, making jokes. They couldn't find Jerry, so the three of them got into a cab and left together, a trio of masculine shoulders filling the paned-in back seat with gruff laughter and blurted comments.

He entered his dark, narrow-halled apartment in a grainy mental state. He stopped briefly before the toilet on his way to bed. He stripped off his clothes and dropped them in the middle of the floor. He lay on his back and put one hand on his cock. He imagined dozens of intriguing images, perusing the possible nuance of each circumstance. There was Cecilia. There was the girl at the bar. There was Sara. "Get my belt," he had said to her. She hesitated. "Don't you think you deserve it?" He masturbated watching spread-legged Sara arch her neck and rub her injured-looking vagina. He finished. He mopped his abdomen with a "snot rag." A memory separated from the fantasy and lingered.

"I love you," said Sara.

"It's not real," he said. "It's puppy love."

"No. I love you." She nuzzled his cheek with her nose and lips, and her tenderness pierced him.

The image became tiny and unnaturally white, was surrounded by darkness, then faded like the picture on a turned-off TV.

Connection

Susan had not been in Manhattan for five years, and she had been looking forward to this visit as a gorgeous wallow in sentimentality and the mild pain of déjà vu. The first three days had been just that. She had gone on long walks, visited with old friends and sat in cafés she'd once frequented as a thin, long-haired girl, lonely and worrying over tea. She had wandered through these days desultorily, enjoying the odd mix of memories and emotions that playfully showed their shadows and vanished again.

She had been walking on Bleecker toward Lafayette when a tiny, youthful bag lady entered her vision. She was standing still in the middle of the sidewalk, one hand out, the other daintily holding a small plastic garbage bag as though it were a pocketbook, begging from everyone and looking at no one. Her torn sweater, ragged skirt and wool socks were drably color-coordinated; her small head was tilted at an odd birdlike angle that was an unintentional caricature of childlike curiosity. Her clearly once-beautiful face was as still as her body; her full lips, potentially so expressive, were held fixed and tight. Her stillness amidst the march of New Yorkers made her look lost and groundless, but there was an intensity about her, and a feeling of heat, as though she were exuding some sticky substance from her pores. The quick feeling of panic in Susan's stomach made her turn and walk the other way before she had a mental reaction; when she figured out why she was upset, she felt even worse. The bag lady looked exactly like Leisha, her best friend many years ago. Her face, posture, even the style of her rags recalled Leisha.

Susan turned a corner and stopped against a wall, her heart beat-

ing miserably. She remembered an article or a talk show or something where a smug somebody discussed the problem of chance
meetings with old friends who were not as successful as you, and
how you could avoid rubbing it in. She thought: This could not be
Leisha. She had not seen or spoken to Leisha since their unhappy
falling-out six years ago. The last time Susan had heard from her
was when she received an invitation to Leisha's wedding (she was
marrying an attorney at a country club), which Susan had scorn-
fully thrown in the trash. Surely even Leisha couldn't have gone
from being a well-off wife to a bag lady in six years. And even if she
had, she had a middle-class family ready (and alert for just this purpose) to sweep her into its bosom. Still, anything was possible, and,
as Leisha herself had constantly pointed out, she was very unstable.
She was unskilled except as a waitress, and Susan had always worried about what would happen to her once she lost her beauty.

Turning the corner wasn't simply a selfish desire to avoid unpleasantness; Susan could imagine the pain that Leisha would feel if
she was recognized, and it made her cringe. But she would have to
get her off the street, buy her a meal, get in touch with her family
and so on. She acknowledged and then stifled the idea that her old
friend might be too disturbed to remember her, and was appalled to
suddenly identify a part of herself that was satisfied, even pleased,
at the thought of Leisha the bag lady. This part of her wanted to
help Leisha, but only out of duty and the pleasure of condescen-
sion; their friendship had ended angrily. Susan dropped her head
and covered her face with her hands, raising it to the gawking gaze
of a passing teenager.

She stepped into the sidewalk march again, and the bag lady
was gone. No, there she was, standing against the wall. Susan
walked right up to her and started to speak, then realized that the
woman wasn't Leisha. The stranger looked at her with mild, glassy
eyes (hazel, not dark brown) and put out her hand. Relieved but
disconcerted, Susan groped through her purse, found five dollars
and pressed it into the pinched little hand. The woman put it away
without looking at it and said, "Jesus loves you."

Susan walked back to her friend's apartment via Eighth Street, becoming depressed as she was reminded of expeditions with Leisha for shoes. Leisha had been part of an amorphous body of memories provoked by this visit to Manhattan, but now she was the lens through which all the other memories were seen, Susan cursed her impressionability and tried to think of something else.

Susan was thirty-five years old, and Leisha thirty-four. When they were friends, Susan was an aspiring writer and Leisha an actress. Whenever she had a positive image of Leisha—a rarity during these last six years—she saw them together in Leisha's apartment drinking tea, drinking wine, snorting coke, something, and talking about their careers. Leisha had loved the word "career." "I think it's going to happen for you really first," she'd say. "Like *boom*, your career's just going to skyrocket—I mean it."

It hadn't. Susan had spent most of her New York years typing, proofreading or coat-checking, selling an article maybe twice a year. Little by little she had given up trying to make it as a writer and had taken an entry-level position with a journal that she didn't think much of. Her editorial career didn't exactly skyrocket, but it puttered along nicely. In Chicago, where she lived now, she edited a pretentious TV magazine and occasionally wrote film reviews for a local entertainment guide that paid almost nothing but gave her a chance to pontificate about aesthetics. When she thought about the magazine, she despised it and considered herself a failure; when she didn't think about it, she would catch herself enjoying the work and decide that it was where she belonged.

"And what do you think will happen with *my* career?" Leisha would ask, pulling back her shoulders and revealing her long, alert neck. Susan had answered her cautiously and it had been just as well. Leisha had taken the same acting course repeatedly for three years until the teacher told her she couldn't take it anymore. She'd had one showcase, a string of auditions and then spent the next few years wringing her hands, seeing therapists and going into debt on her charge cards.

Susan passed the Eighth Street Theater and noted the long-haired boys in black pants hanging around the entrance in a communal slouch. She remembered when she and Leisha would stand outside the St. Marks Bar and Grill in the summer wearing black Capri pants and white lipstick. She snapped her tongue against the roof of her mouth, making the classic junior-high-schooler's noise of contempt for her own sentimentality, then remembered that sentiment was what her visit to New York was all about.

She walked up Greenwich Avenue, scanning the Korean fruit stands that she had always liked so much, the tiny hardware stores selling toylike, largely superfluous wares, the cafés with tense outdoor patios and waiters racing to classical music with prim, neurotic steps. It was almost nauseatingly rich compared to clean, terse Chicago. She admired the swaggering young women in their sweaters and leather jackets and the aloof-faced men with arrogant hip-twitching gaits. She imagined Leisha walking with her in a tweed jacket and short black boots, a tiny spike-haired girl with an odd beeline walk and an intent, condensed quality illuminating her angular face.

They had met when they were college students in Ann Arbor. Both had been involved in brief affairs with the same man, who unfortunately turned out to be an uninteresting swine, something that took each of them an unduly long time to realize. Leisha had been the first; he had met Susan only a month after they broke up. She'd become aware of Leisha at a party given by his roommate, Leisha's then-current lover. Susan had been standing against a wall in the dark, drinking vodka from a plastic cup and watching this theatrical little creature flap drunkenly around a clearly more sober partner on the dance floor, all elbows, jerking hips and senseless knee-bending dips. Her partner suddenly hoisted her up and solemnly circled the room, holding her aloft over his head like a sacrifice as she squeaked, "Give me a break, Eliot, pulease!" Susan disliked her immediately. She thought: I'm a much better dancer, and, putting her drink on the windowsill, went to demonstrate it. (Much later she learned that Leisha hadn't thought much of her dancing either. "It was like, okay, what does a girl do when she dances? She rotates her hips and sticks out her breasts a lot and *un*dulates.")

Susan was aware of her intermittently after that—at parties, coffee shops, movies or walking at a distance with her stiff-hipped, mobile-necked poodle walk. She would hear Leisha's name mentioned in gossip, usually in a tone of amused tolerance and in the context of some blighted romance, with the word "crazy" figuring prominently. Then Susan became friendly with a girl named Alex, who was, coincidentally, sharing a house with Leisha and another girl. Alex didn't like Leisha either; she and Susan loved to talk about how trivial and fake she was.

But this talk began to have an unexpected effect. As they disparaged and analyzed Leisha, a strange affection for her began to manifest itself. They started to say things like, "Well, she's an asshole, but you have to admit she has a good heart." When Susan saw her on the street, she regarded her as a character in a movie, a mysterious figure who might or might not reveal herself. Her reputed excesses and romantic fiascoes began to appeal to Susan. Her overblown gestures seemed like the gaudy plumage of something too refined and frail to appear unadorned. Besides, morbid, serious Susan, who would brood with a bespectacled roommate for hours over tea and toast when a romance collapsed, could not help but feel a kind of admiration for this person who ran around town chattering about the most embarrassing and painful situations as though she were discussing a musical comedy. It was vulgar, but there was a bravado to it that Susan began to sentimentalize against her will. (In fact, she did discover later that Leisha was very fragile, and that she was usually reacting to a nasty scene that some boy or other had already made public before she ever opened her mouth, that her hysterical tattling was thus a form of self-defense.)

This burgeoning interest in her finally found expression when Leisha got pregnant—for the third time, said Alex. She was in bed with the flu and morning sickness when Alex and Susan went to visit her. She was sitting up in her dishevelled bed in an old blue velveteen robe, surrounded by fashion magazines and sodas, her brown eyes lively and alert. She looked at Susan with discomforting but flattering intensity. Susan sat on the bed. "I heard you were sick. I thought I'd come to see how you were doing."

They talked about leather gloves, high heels and their favorite writers. It was the first time that Susan had ever really heard Leisha's voice—the quick, low-pitched voice affected by a certain type of teenage sex star in the fifties and picked up again by bouffant-haired singers in the seventies, only in Leisha it had an intelligent edge that was not ironic but somehow plain and comforting, as if, honey, she'd been there and back, and she knew how important it was just to sit and have a drink and a good talk—which now seemed like a ridiculous affectation in a twenty-one-year-old college student. Susan realized that almost anything you talked about with this girl would seem important. And it appeared that Leisha was having a similar reaction to her. It was, as Leisha said later, the time they fell in love.

After Leisha had her third abortion, they began spending time together. They met ritualistically for brunch at the Dialtone Café on Sundays so they could discuss whatever had happened the night before, or rant about whatever they'd been obsessed with the previous week.

"The thing that drives me nuts about it is that Elena—well, she's just a twat. She really is." Leisha was talking about a party they'd been to, during which a recent ex of hers had disappeared into the bedroom with a South American. "He thinks she's so exotic because she's twenty-six and she's been married and she's from South America, but I've seen her and she's nothing special. She's just passive and quiet and looks totally ordinary. He probably thinks she's got a lot going for her because she's a law student and I'm not directed yet. But I know I'm as interesting as she is and when I figure out what I want to do . . . I don't know." She picked up her fork, put it down, pulled at the back of her hair and wrapped her arms around her shoulders in the straightjacket position that she assumed when she was upset.

Susan could actually remember her response: "I'm so sick and tired of hearing the words 'directed' and 'career,' I could scream."

"But you do want a career, don't you?"

"No. I want to work at Dunkin' Donuts when I get out of school. I want to get fat. Or be addicted to heroin. I want to be a disaster."

"Why? Oh, you're joking. But I know what you mean. I'm sick

of these closed-minded career people too. It's just that I'm getting tired of feeling like a stupid . . . well, a stupid cunt. I want to do something with my talent. I know I've got talent."

Susan ate her toast and stared at her, loving her, almost gloating over her. She loved her tiny fingers, her hot face, her bright nervous energy, her pathetic assertion that she had talent. That she talked like the worst stereotype of the girliest girl imaginable only enhanced her appeal. Susan could not explain this perverse love to herself, but there it was. Perhaps it was so strong because she had almost no other female friends in college; most of her emotional energy had been spent on men—she'd had fewer affairs than Leisha but spent twice the time brooding over them. Maybe the extremities and obviousness of a cartoon girl were all that she could handle in another woman. It was probably for this reason that Leisha chose to be a cartoon girl, she thought sadly.

The curious thing was, Leisha had loved Susan too, at least initially, as another kind of caricature. Susan had been surprised to hear that for months she'd been a source of jealousy and speculation, that Leisha had been deeply puzzled by this solemn, self-contained and (to Leisha) weirdly silent girl. Besides, Susan had quite a reputation in Ann Arbor herself, thanks to their mutual boyfriend. "She's nothing like she looks," he'd say to anyone who'd listen. "She's kinky as hell." Then he'd generously explain how and in what ways, somehow managing to leave his kinkiness out.

"You remind me of black stiletto heels," Leisha had said. "I used to picture you all in black, in stretch pants and spike-heeled shoes."

"Oh, brother," said Susan. But she was flattered.

The apartment Susan was staying in belonged to an old friend named Bobby, who was in Europe for the month and hadn't bothered to arrange a sublet for so short a time. It was located in the Village only a few blocks from the apartment she had lived in for most of her time in Manhattan. It was much larger than her old apartment, and brighter.

Her apartment in Chicago was even larger than Bobby's. It

had high ceilings and large windows; it was fashionably decorated with soft colors and spare-limbed furnishings. It was kept clean by a weekly maid. She had attractive kitchen accessories in matching colors. She remembered Leisha visiting her tiny Manhattan studio and laughing at her, incredulous that after four months Susan's utensils were still limited to two forks, a knife and a spoon.

She went into Bobby's bedroom and looked at herself in the long mirror, a plump woman wandering calmly toward middle age, standing with one arm wrapped around her waist and a drink in her hand. She had never thought she would be plump or calm. Ten years ago, even six years ago, she never gained weight, no matter how much she ate. Her sudden plumpness was such a novelty that she enjoyed it rather than fighting it, as did most women her age. "You've finally come into your real . . . look," her mother said approvingly. "You're not a skinny kid anymore." This late maternal acceptance had pleased her to such an extent that she found it somewhat sad; just a few years earlier she would've rejected it as the words of a woman glad to see the last of an unreasonable reminder of youth and insouciance in the form of her unusually slender daughter.

Her life in New York had been erratic and unconnected. She had lived hand to mouth most of the time, working a series of menial jobs that made her feel isolated and unseen, yet strangely safe. She ate dinners of rice and beans or boxes of Chinese takeout food on the floor. She stayed up until seven or eight in the morning working on her manuscripts, and then slept all day. She went to Harlem to interview voodoo practitioners. She went to nightclubs and after-hours bars, standing on the periphery of scene after scene with Leisha or some other, less central girlfriend. She took long walks late at night, especially in winter, loving the sound of her own muted footfalls, the slush-clogged city noises, and the sight of the bundled, shuffling drunks staggering home, looking up in surprise to see a young woman walking alone at 4:00 A.M. The desolation and cruelty of the city winter horrified and fascinated her. She was astonished by the contrasting layers of existence sitting so closely atop one another, and the desperate survival of bag people and mis-

fits wedged into the comfortless air pockets and crawl spaces between layers. During her first year in the city she gave spare change
to anyone who asked her. Eventually she gave money only if she
happened to have some in her hand when she was asked.

Her relationships with men at that time were disturbing; she had
conversation after conversation with Leisha, agonizing over why
she always wound up with these terrible people. She remembered
them all in an embarrassing blur: the pretty, delicate drug addict,
the masochistic Chinese boy, the pretentious Italian journalist, the
married professor, the pompous law student, the half-crazy club
owner who almost strangled her one night with his belt. The guy
she met and screwed in the rest room of some tiny East Village
bar, the one who later involved her in an exhausting ménage à trois
with his Italian girlfriend. Leisha had violently (and primly, Susan
thought) disapproved of that one. Strangely enough, after fleeing
what she contemptuously labeled "conventional" and "suburban"
for anything "unconventional" she could safely lay her hands on,
Leisha had performed an indignant and sudden about-face, calling
the bohemia she'd adopted "pretentious" and "fake." When Susan
didn't follow, Leisha had said things like "It's just horribly painful
to even be around you when you're involved in this adolescent,
self-destructive garbage."

It was too bad Leisha couldn't see her now, with her steady job,
her matching housewares, her kind and gentle boyfriend. It was
also annoying to know that Leisha would come to some happy
conclusion about her based on the current trappings of her life
("How wonderful it is that Susan has become so stable") and then
compare her favorably with the younger Susan. Susan examined
her clearly lined face as she stood before the mirror. There had
been changes in her during the last six years, and she thought most
of them were good. But she was still, for better or worse, the same
woman who had drunkenly screwed a stranger in the reeking can
of a tacky bar and then run out into a cab, smiling as she pressed
her phone number into his hand.

She sighed and went into the "living area," leaning against an
exposed brick wall to look out a curtainless window. It seemed as

though her friendship with Leisha had never been what she would now call a friendship at all, but a complex system of reassurance and support for self-involved fantasies that they had propped up between them and reflected back and forth. Susan now identified her early fascination with Leisha as a vicarious erotic connection with the ex-lover they had both slept with. She did not fantasize about Leisha and this man together, but she had been oddly gratified to experience secondhand the dynamic between him and this throaty-voiced little bad girl, and to reflect this dynamic back to Leisha, making it more of a drama by becoming another character in the story. Leisha had done the same, clearly enjoying her two-way link with their lover and the mysterious, contrary, perverse woman he had described to her, this tackily glamorous icon of a dirty-magazine woman who was also her reliable friend Susan. During the first year of their friendship they discussed and described him, pro and con, right down to the blond pinkness, the raised, strangely exposed quality of his genitals, and they were both greatly amused to discover that the sight of them talking and giggling together unnerved him.

She had dinner that night with her old friend Barbara. They went to a restaurant on Bleecker Street that served neat little dinners to predictably soothing music. Barbara was a jeweler who had never quite been able to become a big name in the industry, but whose work was a persistent presence in fashion magazines and department stores. She had recently separated from her husband of twelve years, a sculptor whom Susan had known. Barbara didn't seem so much upset by the separation as appalled.

"I can't say that suddenly we didn't know each other, or anything like that, because I actually know John very well. It isn't even that we don't love each other anymore, because I do love John, even if it's more of a sisterly love at this point. People say that it gets that way after you've been married awhile." She cut her salmon steak into pieces with polite, relaxed moves, as though pausing in a discussion of art or film.

"Well, what is it, do you think?" asked Susan.

Barbara sat back. "I'm not sure how to describe it. It was like everything that supported the relationship was coming from the outside. Judging by all the signs, we were a perfectly successful couple and John was an ideal husband for me—rich, blond, tall, sensitive, ad nauseam. But even worse, it seemed as if our most intimate conversations were based on what we were supposed to be saying, and what we were supposed to be. Nothing seemed to come directly from us. Do you know what I mean? I sound like a hippie, I know."

"No, I know what you mean."

"I don't know. I didn't see it that way at the time. He was just driving me crazy and I guess I was driving him crazy too."

"I don't know anymore how much a relationship can be based on what comes from the inside," said Susan. "With Steve and me, it's all based on us, and it's very genuine and very sweet but sometimes it seems as if we're involved in a fantasy that has nothing to do with the real world. Maybe there's nothing wrong with that, I don't know, but it can begin to feel solipsistic." She remembered what her father had said to her during an argument when she was fifteen years old: "You want to suck people dry, you expect them to pour out their guts to you and you to them over and over and over until you know everything, and it just doesn't work that way. Relationships are built from 'Hi, how are you doing?' and 'I'm fine.'" He had said this last word like a stake was being driven through his heart.

"Do you remember Leisha?"

"I sure do. The nutty one with the musician boyfriend. Why?"

"I thought I saw her on the street today. There was this bag lady who looked just like her."

"Oh, my God."

"I didn't realize that it wasn't her until I was an inch from her face."

"What did you do?"

"Gave her five dollars."

• • •

She lay on Bobby's futon and thought of Steve. He was a quiet man whom she considered brilliant. He worked in the public relations department of a magazine neither one respected. They saw each other almost every night, they had keys to each other's apartment. They had private jokes and several cute nicknames apiece. Sometimes it seemed as if they spoke a language foreign to other people, that there was something closeted and defeated in their closeness. But they made each other happy. There was, in magazine-speak, a "real connection." She opened her eyes. "Connection" was a vague word when applied to humans. What did it mean? She remembered a man she'd had a short affair with before she'd met Steve. He was a sweet, practical person who never read books, rarely went out, and didn't seem to care strongly about anything except a few close friends and a martial art he practiced with fanatic zeal. They had nothing in common. In most ways he bored her. Yet when she touched him she felt a sensitivity in his body, a sense of receptivity that she rarely encountered in men. When he held her against his chest, she felt secure and protected in a way that had nothing to do with his muscular body. She felt that they were nourishing each other in some important, invisible way. But they could barely hold a conversation.

At times she had thought that this was the only kind of connection you could have with people—intense, inexplicable and ultimately incomplete. During the months that her friendship with Leisha was beginning to wane, she would think, Well, I can't talk to her and I don't respect her, but she has a beauty that can perhaps only be appreciated on a nonintellectual level. Like a sudden flame of piercing movement in an unexceptional dancer, or the grace and spirit of an animal.

She remembered them walking down St. Marks together doing an acting-class exercise. One person would say something and the other person would repeat it, with slight changes in words or expression. Susan thought it was pointless, but Leisha loved the exercise.

"I love to walk down the street and look at people," began Leisha.

"You love to walk down the street looking at people."

"People look at me when I walk down the street."

"You like it when people look at you."

"You like it when people look at you."

"I'm scared when people look at me."

"I'm scared when people look at me."

"But you like it."

"Do you like it?"

"It makes me nervous and I pull my earrings."

"You pull your earrings all the time."

"I hate to pull my earrings."

"I want to pet your earrings."

"You want to pet my earrings."

It was like nursery rhymes; they were two cute girls walking down the street talking harmless nonsense, while all around them the world was in full operation. Desperate vendors displayed miserable items arranged on dirty blankets—T-shirts, ratty sweaters and vinyl belts, wrinkled old magazines, faded books and records. Garbage flapped in the streets and humans walked up and down the sidewalks, on their way to perform hundreds of actions in a remarkably orderly fashion. The sun was evenly warm and pleasant and it seemed as though this was all that anyone could expect out of life. Susan felt an ache of futile tenderness for Leisha and she impulsively reached out and stroked her four serial earrings the way she would pet a cat.

It was sometime during her second year in New York that their conversations began to seem like frantic attempts to wring each other for support that neither could give. Leisha became involved with an abusive rock musician. She called Susan, it seemed, only when she was hysterical in a phone booth after a fight with him. When he left her for a singer, Leisha went to Bellevue, was discharged, slit her wrists, went home to Michigan and returned in a state of quasi-hysteria that remained constant for the rest of the time Susan knew her. She immediately moved back in with the musician, who had been dumped by the singer. She was dropped by most of her Michigan friends, who said that she was too self-indulgent and theatrical to cope with. Susan didn't know if what they said was true or not, but it seemed unkind. She wanted to remain loyal to Leisha, but she was floundering so thoroughly herself that when they talked they seemed like drowning people clinging to each other for life.

The first time the musician walked out, Leisha called her at five in the morning, sobbing and pleading with her to come over. Susan got out of bed and took a cab down to Eighth Street, where ghostly men and women were tipping over garbage cans to better examine the contents. She sat in Leisha's grandly rumpled, granule-ridden bed, holding her tight in her arms, as though the pressure of her grip should equal the intensity of Leisha's trembling. "I feel so empty, Susan, I feel so rotten and empty inside." Susan kissed her forehead and stroked her hair and held her until her arms were sore, but she did not know what to say. Eventually, Leisha's trembling subsided and she slept, and Susan sat completely still, watching some fat, hideous pigeons stump around on a neighbor's filthy window ledge while Leisha's skin became stuck to hers and her limbs went gradually numb. Why did Leisha feel empty? What did empty mean? What should exist in Leisha that didn't? Was it a quality that other people had? She tried to imagine what Leisha looked like inside and pictured a set of dull-colored wires, some dead, others short-circuited and flickering in the dark, discharging a profusion of heat and bright color that sparked wildly, blew fuses and went dead.

There were more of these calls and Susan began to resent them, particularly because when Susan needed someone to talk to Leisha would not return her calls. Leisha was too upset, it seemed, to do anything but fight with the musician, but she liked having Susan available as a witness. Susan felt like an accessory, especially when Leisha invited her to a dinner party that ended with Leisha and the musician flinging pasta and otherwise slugging it out while a plump drummer tried vainly to separate them. Eventually he left her for the singer again and Leisha began seeing someone else. Sometimes the three of them would go out, but the evenings would invariably conclude with Leisha drunk in a phone booth, screaming at the musician's answering machine while her new boyfriend stared into space.

The really annoying thing about this was that just as Susan was getting ready to tell Leisha that she was feeling used, Leisha told her that she felt Susan only called her when she was depressed. Susan was flabbergasted and outraged, and so was Leisha when Susan told her why. They didn't speak for almost a year. It was apparently during this time that Leisha finally got rid of the musician and began dating the lawyer.

The friendship resumed when they ran into each other on the street and found that they couldn't stop talking. They began having lunch. Leisha grimaced and shrugged her shoulders and said "I don't know" a lot when she talked about her acting. She said that she wanted to have a baby. When they walked down Eighth Street she would say, "Oh, don't you hate these people with their standard-issue green hair standing straight up?"

"No," said Susan.

"But it is so passé, I mean, can't they do anything else?"

"I think teenagers need these things."

Susan refrained from pointing out that barely a year ago Leisha's hair also had stood straight up, but soon they argued about other things.

"We have to talk," said Susan, and they met in a cappuccino bar frantically decorated with annoying statuettes and candelabras.

"I feel drained by you," said Leisha. "Every time I'm around you I feel like you're hanging on to me, that there's something you want and I don't know what it is, and I can't stand it."

"I don't know what you're talking about. All I want from you is friendship. If you feel drained by that, there's nothing I can do."

"Maybe some of this is old stuff, because you seem more positive now than you did before, but I still feel the effects of those phone conversations we used to have when you would call me and say that you felt like dying."

"Wait a minute. Don't you remember when you'd call *me* at six A.M. and tell me that I had to come over right away or you were going to kill yourself?"

"You used to tell me that you didn't see how people could stand to live. Any people."

"Oh, Jesus Christ, this is stupid. Who was the one who started all those depressing conversations, Leisha? You did, after—" She started to say "you went into Bellevue" and couldn't.

"I'm not saying it was all your fault, and don't try to tell me it was all mine, because it wasn't. It was this strange dynamic that somehow got started between us. We got turned into these sob sisters and I don't know how it happened. I don't know what happened to us, Susan. It was never like that in Ann Arbor." Leisha's round eyes were full of an unreadable emotion.

"I didn't mind giving you support," said Susan. "But it was always the same thing, always Eddie and you. It didn't matter what I said, you never listened to me anyway. And if you didn't want to talk about Eddie, you never called just to talk to me. You wouldn't even return my calls. You even got Eddie to tell me you weren't home when you were. He told me."

"Oh, Susan, I was sick then, don't you understand? I slit my wrists, remember? I was a sick, worthless piece of shit." Her voice faltered; Susan recognized the prelude to tears.

"You weren't a piece of shit," mumbled Susan.

"And anyway, I feel like you're doing the same thing to me now."

"What?"

"All we ever talk about is you. You don't seem interested in my relationship with Jonathan or my wedding or my therapy. Those are the things I'm doing in my life. I'm trying very hard to get well and to have a good relationship and get married." Her voice became a tremulous squeak, tears appeared, her face crumpled delicately and she pecked at it with her napkin.

Susan scowled at her cold cup of chamomile tea. She couldn't bring herself to say that she despised Jonathan, that she thought their relationship was a farce, that she hated traditional weddings and that she thought Leisha used therapy the same way she had used Eddie—to distract herself from her own life. A wave of classical music surged through the room, loudly enough to knock over a table, aggressively soothing the eaters of cannoli and cute cakes.

"And the way you talk about Stef all the time—"

Stef was the man Susan had met in a public rest room. "I don't talk about Stef all the time."

"It seems like you do. And what you say is so horrible, even if you talk about him a little it's a lot."

How could we have pretended to be friends for so long, Susan thought.

"Especially when you talk about him and that Italian girl, it's so awful it makes me hurt inside. Don't you see how they're using you?"

"They're not using me," Susan said stiffly.

"Oh no, what about the time they tried to shoot you up in the bathroom at Area, or wherever the fuck you were?"

"They didn't shoot me up."

"They tried."

"Not very hard, obviously. Anyway, it doesn't matter if they're using me, I don't care. I'm doing this thing with them because I want to. I can take care of myself, and I'm not trying to make you a part of it."

"But when you tell me stories like that nipple-piercing thing, you *are* making me part of it. Why do you put yourself in positions where you have to take care of yourself?"

They stared at each other with what seemed painfully close to hate. A raw feeling traveled up Susan's throat. She was sweating.

Leisha spoke slowly and deliberately. "I think you're involved with them because you don't have anything else to do. I think you think it's *interesting*." This last word was sarcastic enough for two or three words. "And it's not interesting at all. It is sordid and disgusting." Her nostrils dilated.

"How dare you?" said Susan. "How dare you judge me?"

Susan opened her eyes and contemplated the maniacal outline of a feathered hat hanging on Bobby's coatrack. In retrospect she had to admit that part of her anger had come from the element of truth in Leisha's last accusation. But Stef and Anna *had* been interesting to her at the time; and anyway, how dare she indeed?

Susan turned over in bed. Their fantasies had changed, their tastes in props had diverged, and neither one could satisfy the other's needs any longer. Since what they were inside didn't matter, they separated. Susan had ended a chapter in her life, and doubtless it had felt the same to Leisha, who probably saw their friendship as a symbol of bad living and delusion. Leisha had sent Susan the engraved wedding invitation a week after their discussion. ("The honor of your presence is requested at the marriage of . . .") Susan had said "How beautiful" to her empty apartment and summarily shredded the card.

Susan turned over again. Still, she wished she knew where Leisha was. She would like to talk to her. She remembered the time they had gone dancing one summer. They had danced for hours in a hot, damp place, until they collapsed in each other's arms, Leisha's small, sweating, palpitating chest pressed against hers. She remembered having the almost tangible sensation that they were creatures with delicate invisible feelers waving between them, sending tenderness and warmth from one to the other.

She sat up and turned on the bedside light. She could reach Leisha. She probably still had friends in Manhattan who knew where she was. After a minute's thought, she remembered the last names of two of Leisha's friends. Dialing information, she discovered that one of them no longer lived in the city and the other was unlisted. She called the restaurant where Leisha had worked; it was still open, but no one remembered her. The only possibility was the man they had both dated; the last Susan had heard, he was living in New York, but they hadn't spoken for years and it was after two o'clock in the morning. She had to pace the room for fifteen minutes before she developed the courage to call. When he finally answered he was too surprised to be nasty, until she asked him if he knew where Leisha was.

"I really don't know. I heard that they moved to Los Angeles a couple of years ago, but that might've been a rumor. You called me at two-thirty in the morning to ask about Leisha?"

She hung up rather gratified that she'd slighted and irritated him. She paced a bit more and then settled down in the living area, where she stared into space. She remembered a story she'd read once in which the main character, an older woman who was pining to see a boy she'd likely never see again, found accidental solace in late-night TV, where she saw an actor who looked like an older version of her young heartthrob. Leisha had, after all, wanted to be an actress at one point. Susan found the remote-control unit and flicked on the TV. It was on the pornographic cable station. No one there resembled Leisha. Neither did anyone on *Get Smart, Love That Bob* or the Japanese horror movie. The last channel she tried revealed a nameless old Italian thing about international espionage, which had a murky, kinky sexual flavor that held her interest for several minutes. And, in fact, there was a dark, intense woman who was playing an intellectual slut. If Leisha had ever become an actress, this was probably the kind of role she'd get, but Susan doubted she had the tenacity to land roles even like this one.

She flicked off the TV. It embarrassed her to hold such a low opinion of Leisha's ability, but it wasn't a reflection of contempt. Leisha was simply meant to feel and be, not to do. But what an arrogant thing to close off Leisha's possibilities like that. After all, no one who knew Susan six years before could have predicted exactly where she would wind up, and some people had been surprised.

She put her head back on the couch and closed her eyes. She imagined Leisha as an actress in a sci-fi movie, playing a tiny queen in silver lamé. She saw her as a mother in a blue-and-white checked blouse, kneeling on the floor to play a game with her child. She saw her as an aging hipster in a bar, her eyes made up in flames of black and silver, complaining about her current relationship to whoever would listen. She saw her as a bag lady. Then the images peeled away and she saw her standing in empty space, wearing the tight Capri pants she used to wear, a dreamy, half-smiling girl, her intensity momentarily muted by some inner reflection. She looked at this girl and realized that, with all the falseness and silliness between them, she had cared for her, and been cared for in return. She wanted to talk to her, and tomorrow she would try again. She sat in the living area for almost an hour thinking about what she might say to her, and what Leisha might say back.

Trying to Be

STEPHANIE WASN'T A "professional lady" exactly; tricking was just something she slipped into, once a year or so, when she was feeling particularly revolted by clerical work, or when she couldn't pay her bills. She even liked a few of her customers, but she had never considered dating one; she kept her secret forays into prostitution neatly boxed and stored away from her real life. She was thus a little dismayed to find herself standing in high heels and underwear in front of the smeared mirror in the "Shadow Room," handing her phone number to Bernard the lawyer. She felt she was being drawn deeper into something she had no business doing in the first place, but she had no boyfriend, she liked the lawyer and, since he was married, it seemed likely he would leave only a faint impression on her life.

She had been working at her current "house" for three nights when she met him. It wasn't as posh or expensive as the other two places she'd worked, but it was comfortable and safe. She hadn't wanted to go back to the first place because of the peculiarity of the manager, who'd read the girls' auras daily and made them chant over anointed candles in the kitchen to "purify the space"; and she couldn't go back to the second because it had been closed by the Mafia. She wasn't well connected or knowledgeable enough to systematically search for the best establishment, so she had settled for this—a run-down townhouse apartment with poor ventilation and sad old smells coiling through the rooms. It was called "Christine's" after the woman who ran it, a tiny frantic blond tyrant who rather desperately fancied her hideous paisley sitting room to be a salon and forced long minutes of excruciating conversation between women and johns before allowing them to escape up the stairs. "We're known for our intellectual women," she told Stephanie during her interview. "Everybody here does something. Alana here is an artist. Suzie is a fashion designer and Beatrice is a nurse," The three women on the couch regarded Stephanie blankly. Christine gave Stephanie the working name "Perry" and told her to wear something in which she could "meet her mother for lunch and then rendezvous with her boyfriend for cocktails." This ridiculous pretense, teetering pathetically toward aspiration, appealed to her. She thought: It's only for a few weeks, and showed up two days later in a tight silver minidress.

She had come downstairs, after being summoned through the intercom to "meet someone," hurried and disheveled, one stocking badly run, having left her portly, huffing client to finish his ablutions alone. She stood before the new man, feeling slightly knock-kneed in her short black skirt, smiling goofily and thinking, for some reason, of the *I Love Lucy* show. The canned laughter mumbled as Christine folded her hands and asked, "Well, Bernard, would you like to see Perry?"

The man stood up and said, "Yes, very much." He was about forty-five, very tall and thin, and wore an absurd bow tie with his conservative suit. He had kind eyes and an intelligent, inquisitive demeanor. She felt that something about her genuinely excited him, and she was flattered.

He followed her to the awful burgundy Shadow Room. He stripped and lay on the bed, his torso resting against a pillow, his slender naked body placidly expectant, his almost alarmingly large penis lying half-hard on his thigh. She took off her high heels and knelt beside him on the bed. He didn't touch her or even move closer, he just lay there and looked at her as though he were waiting to be amused. The old air conditioner moaned and dripped.

"I like your hair," he said. "It's a becoming style."

She self-consciously ruffled her spiky, black-dyed crew cut. "Oh, it's fashionable now. Lots of women have this cut."

"Yes, I know. But it suits you especially well."

She said thank you and pulled her shirt over her head.

He glanced at her breasts with apparent approval but still made no move to touch her.

She decided with some relief that he was a talker and settled into conversation

She quickly found out that he worked for the city on the re-development of the Lower East Side, that he did not love his wife, though he was very fond of her, and that they rarely made love. He stayed with her because he didn't want to be alone.

"And what about you? What do you do when you're not at this place?"

She grimaced. "Well, I don't know if I do anything. I'm trying to become a writer. That's why I came to New York." She paused, wondering if that sounded ridiculous to this man who wore suits and patronized prostitutes. "Do you think that's stupid?"

"No, not at all. Why would I think it's stupid?"

"Because so many girls in these houses have the desire to do something else, but it's obvious that in most cases they don't have any talent or are too scared, and I don't know, it just seems sort of pathetic to me. I don't even tell people here what I do. I say I'm a secretary or a dental technical or something."

"But that's silly. As it happens, I know there have been some very talented people working here. There was a whole coterie of various artists at one point. One of them was a performance artist who went off to Italy and started working with, oh, some avant-garde choreographer—I know the name but I can't think of it. Anyway, I hear she's doing fine."

"How do you know?"

"I was a regular of hers, and we saw each other on the outside. She had short hair like yours, only hers was orange." He smiled, as though this disclosed a revealing element that firmly established a relationship between Stephanie and the orange-haired girl. "As a matter of fact, she used this place to collect material for her work. She was extremely bright and very aware of all the contradictions she embodied by being here." He smiled gently. "She could talk about it endlessly."

She pulled off her skirt and lay down next to him, supporting herself on one elbow. They talked about fiction in *The New Yorker* and *The Atlantic*. She ranted against the trendy writers she despised. They talked about dance performances they'd seen. He described a piece at the Dance Theater Workshop in which the dancers waved large Styrofoam animals at each other and rolled around in paint. She thought it sounded idiotic, but felt tender toward his robustly curious delight in this goofy spectacle.

"I have a Workshop membership and every now and then I get invited to fabulous parties, where all the boys wear long coats and earrings, and all the girls have hair like yours." He beamed.

She thought: At this rate, I'm not going to have to do anything.

They talked about her past, her coldly perfect father, her sad, passive mother, her sister on lithium, her college major, her first romance. He listened gravely. He began to stroke her arm hairs, and then her arm.

He had a seductive touch; she moved closer to him and he put his arms around her. He caressed her as if he were trying to discover the places she most inhabited—not romantically, but tenderly, with a sense of exploration. She was not aroused, exactly, but it was pleasant; it had been a long time since anyone had touched her like this.

She murmured, "The way you touch reminds me of my mother."

"How so?"

"Her touch is very seductive. I don't even like her, but when she starts to touch me, I suddenly become totally vulnerable to her. It's frightening."

He liked this a lot. "That's beautiful," he said.

The intercom buzzed, announcing that they had ten more minutes. She "took care of him" quickly, and they stood to dress. She stuck her feet back in her high heels, and cheerfully tore the sheets off the bed. He zipped up his pants, handed her an extra twenty and told her it had been a relaxing hour. She said yes, actually, it had been for her too, and then trotted off to stuff the wadded-up sheets in a reeking wicker basket. She walked him downstairs, feeling ungainly and knees-out in her tight skirt. She was aware of him looming and lurking darkly behind her as she came under the speculative, moody gaze of three potential Romeos.

"And here's Perry," said Christine brightly.

"Hi," she said, bobbing her head. She turned to Bernard and rolled her eyes as she walked him to the door, knowing that he would enjoy this open display of contempt.

"See you soon," he said. He held her against him for a second, and she experienced a disorienting sense of comfort and safety that made walking back into the invading stares of her prospective boyfriends almost voluptuously exposing. She stood before them, and the canned laughter sounded once more.

That night she went to a group show at a small gallery in Soho that included work by her friend Sandra. As usual, she was one of the few non-artists there. Sandra, nervous and carefully chic in a bright blue pillbox hat and a long black velvet skirt, introduced her as "my friend Stephanie, who writes for *The Village Voice*." This impressed people, even when Stephanie said, "I just wrote one thing for the *Voice* and that was a year and a half ago."

"Yes, but you look like a writer for *The Village Voice*," said a painter.

"That sounds like an insult to me."

"It's not an insult, but it's not a compliment either." He barked out a laugh.

Stephanie attached herself to another conversation about the embarrassing failure of an art gallery that she had never heard of, which, after a rapid shift of participants, became a discussion about somebody's review in the *Times* versus somebody's review in the *Voice*. Sandra rapidly crossed and recrossed the floor, darting in and out of conversations with apparent pleasure and animation. "Nobody's *here*," she hissed finally, near the hors d'oeuvres, even though there were dozens of people present.

Stephanie wandered from conversation to conversation, having an almost panicky feeling that although there were nice, interesting people in the room, the situation, for all its seeming friendliness and ease, precluded her from connecting with the nice and interesting aspects of them. She tried to figure out why this was and could not, beyond the sense that the conversations around her were opening and closing according to the subtle but definite rules that no one had told her about. Then she saw Dara, Sandra's other non-artist friend, standing regally alone. Dara was trying to become a fashion designer, and she looked unusually beautiful that night in a strapless satin dress that was dramatically faded in the middle where someone had probably spilled something on it a long time ago. Stephanie had always admired Dara, even though she was not friendly and had once been very rude to Stephanie on the phone. But Dara seemed pleased to see her and hung on to her presence throughout a shockingly dull conversation that stumbled awkwardly through Sandra's work, Sandra's husband's work, a writer Stephanie liked and a movie. Still, Stephanie resolutely held on to her idea of Dara as an interesting person. She said, "You seem like someone who is at home in the world."

A startled look flared in Dara's eyes; she glanced at Stephanie with disappointment. "Nothing could be further from the truth," she said shortly. "I doubt you know anyone less at home than me."

They stood silently, Stephanie's silence a disheartened one. She had thought she was making a penetrating remark that would impress Dara with her perceptiveness; instead she had revealed herself to be a person living in a dreamworld. This was always happening.

The next day at Christine's, she felt like a person in a dreamworld, specifically a *Playboy* cartoon dreamworld inhabited by beautiful, moronic prostitutes in short pink negligees lolling about on cushions with white cats while large men in suits smiled at them. It was a strangely pleasant sensation. It had been a slow afternoon, and the women lounged on the couch with their high heels off and their feet up, watching TV and eating heavily salted french fries from damp carry-out containers.

Stephanie was talking to Brett, an alert Chinese girl with waist-length hair. Brett had been in "the business" for ten years, since she was seventeen, and she said she was ready to leave. She told story after story about how customers were always trying to take advantage of her, humiliate her or intrude on her sympathies in some grotesque way. "It was just awful," she said, concluding a particularly obnoxious story. "It was as if he'd done it almost, having to listen to him say it, you know?" She leaned forward for a handful of french fries, stuck some in her mouth and chewed meditatively. "When I was younger I had more energy to fight them off. No matter what they said or did, I could keep them away from my real self. But it gets harder and harder and I don't know how much longer I can go on. I want to do something else anyway. I'm bored."

The other women began to talk about the terrible things men had done or tried to do, and how they'd thwarted them or gotten them back. There was a tenacious sense of defended pride in the room, which Stephanie felt both distant from and very much a part of. She thought of how pathetic this pride would seem to someone like Sandra, who had once disgustedly described a brief stint as a cocktail waitress as making her feel "like a whore."

The buzzer rang and Bernard the lawyer appeared, hands in his pockets, a sophisticated fellow playing the part, with mild amusement, of the casual businessman about to enjoy himself with a cheap woman. Stephanie smiled at him and sank back into the couch, feeling she was a sophisticated woman playing cheap. Soon they were back in the Shadow Room.

"Do you remember those cartoons in *Playboy?*" she asked as they lay, not yet touching, on the bed. "The ones about prostitutes with the same faces and bodies lying on pillows, wearing lacy nighties? And the men who were standing with flowers and chocolates in their hands?"

"Yes, of course."

"It's funny, because I used to look at those things when I was ten and eleven years old and—well, I didn't really know what prostitutes were, but it looked like a good thing from what I could see in *Playboy.* They were beautiful and they didn't have to do anything but sit on cushions and men loved them. So I told my mother I wanted to be a prostitute when I grew up."

"That's fabulous." He smiled as though this was the most entertaining thing he'd heard all week.

"Naturally she freaked out, and my parents sent me to a psychiatrist."

"Oh, good Lord."

"But after a few visits the psychiatrist decided I was normal. I mean, I had good grades and friends and everything, so I didn't have to go anymore." She shrugged. "My poor sister wasn't so lucky. He had her on lithium by the time she was eleven."

"But the psychiatrist was wrong about you, wasn't he?"

She laughed, but she thought: He was not wrong. I am actually pretty normal.

"So that's what you're doing. You're playing prostitute." He stroked her face and hair.

She was startled that he seemed to be thinking in the same terms as she had been downstairs. She pictured him with his orange-haired, chain-smoking performance artist, and she had an almost visual sense of his delight in this educated woman who flew in the face of society, deliberately taking on a role that he probably considered demeaning, and then analyzing it. "Actually, I'm not playing. This is for real. I'm not going to give you your money back."

"You know what I mean." He drew her against him and lightly scratched her head.

"But even as a kid I realized there were problems with the customer-hooker romance. Because once, when I was about twelve, I was in my father's study rubbing his neck—I used to do that all the time for him—and there was this *Playboy* calendar over his desk and some babe was on it and I said to him, 'Do you like her?' and he said, 'Sure I do,' and I said, 'Would you like to meet her?' and he looked shocked and said, 'No, she's just a dumb broad.' And I was appalled."

Bernard's smile almost became a laugh. "Well, but you know he was lying. He would've loved to meet her."

"It's not funny. I was hurt by what he said. I was hurt for her."

"No, I know it's not funny. I'm sorry." He lay on top of her and kissed her, cupping her head tenderly in his hands. They kissed and touched each other and then broke apart to talk some more. She told him about the conversation with Brett and how it made her feel. She told him about the opening she had been to the night before, leaving out her almost frightened sense of isolation. She asked what his wife was like.

"She's intelligent, and very independent. She's better at being alone than I am. And she's adventurous in her own way. Last year she went to South America by herself, which isn't something most woman her age would do."

"How old is she?"

"Thirty-nine."

"What does she do?"

"Teaches high school, which she likes very much. I enjoy her, even if it isn't passionate. We actually have separate bedrooms."

"I couldn't be married like that," she said. "There would have to be passion."

"You're very idealistic."

"You're not?"

"No, I'm not. Anyway, marriage isn't about passion for me. We're excellent company for each other. And I don't want to be alone."

They were silent for a moment; she gently felt his earlobes.

"Why do you come to places like this?" she asked.

"Why do you think?"

"I really don't know. How any grown man can accept what happens here as sex is beyond me. You could have affairs if you wanted, I'll bet. You don't seem that interested in sex here, anyway. So why do you come?"

"To meet fascinating creatures I'd never meet in the usual course of my life. Like you." He touched her nose and smiled.

Of course, she realized what he liked about her. He loved the idea of kooky, arty girls who lives "bohemian" lives and broke all the rules. It was the kind of thing he regarded with a certain admiration, but did not want to do himself. He had probably had affairs with eccentric, unpredictable women in college, and then married the most stable, socially desirable woman he could find.

This did not make her feel contempt or draw away from him. She liked this vicarious view of herself; it excited and reassured her. She wasn't a directionless girl adrift in a monstrous city, wandering from one confusing social situation to the next, having stupid affairs. She was a bohemian, experimenting. The idea made rock music start playing in her head. She kissed him with something resembling passion.

"I would like to actually fuck you sometime," he said. "But I don't think you enjoy sex here. I don't want it if you can't enjoy yourself."

She smiled and tweaked the light layer of flab at his waist. "But that doesn't apply to blow jobs, right?"

After he left, the day suddenly became very busy. Most of the men she saw were unpleasant, and she found herself taking refuge in the idea of Bernard the lawyer as she endured their malodorous company.

That night Sandra called her. Stephanie was sitting on her bed eating orange sorbet from a pint box and trying to view her life in a positive way, and she welcomed the interruption.

"Hi," said Sandra. "You're not writing, are you?"

"No, in fact, I was avoiding it."

"Again?"

"I'm afraid so."

Sandra sighed. "Maybe you're trying to write at the wrong time of day. Most people have times of day when they're more productive than others. Have you considered that?"

"No, I haven't. Anyway, I have a job, you know."

"That's right, I forgot. You don't have as much leeway as I do." Sandra was supported by her husband, a painter whose father had given him a building. Stephanie had told Sandra that she was working as a maid for an agency that had several apartments on the Upper West Side. In her mind, this was grubbily close to the truth, and it rendered her conveniently unreachable by phone. She felt that Sandra viewed her fictional job with a mixture of secret repugnance and respect, astounded that a person she knew could do such a job without any apparent loss of self-esteem.

Sandra began to talk about the opening. After Stephanie had left, an important East Village art critic had arrived, and Sandra had hoped he would pay attention to her. But he ignored her completely and openly admired the work done by her friend Yolanda.

"I know it's petty, but by the end of the night, I could hardly speak to her. It's not just this one incident either; she's always getting attention—ever since she started putting those little beads in her hair and going out with that guy Serge. And I know what this sounds like, but sometimes I think people respond to her just because she's black and they want to prove they're not racist. I mean, I know she's good, but I work all the time, and she only does one painting every few months. And her stuff is derivative as hell. I mean, I know everybody's derivative in a way, but you know what I mean. It makes me feel like a piece of shit. Am I being awful?"

"Well . . . sort of," said Stephanie, who thought Yolanda's work was clearly better than Sandra's. "But I understand how you feel." She told Sandra how annoyed she was when the name of a writer she didn't think much of began appearing in bold print in gossip columns everywhere. "When I saw that picture of him in *Vanity Fair* at the Palladium with China Smith, I almost threw up," she said.

They talked about how shallow and fake it all was, and once again Stephanie told the story of the twenty-three-year-old clerk who had driven her to despair with stories of his impending publication in *Esquire* and his subsequent book contract, until she found out that he was certifiably nuts and on lithium, and couldn't possibly be telling the truth.

Stephanie hung up feeling vaguely humiliated. She thought of her job at Christine's, almost so she could feel worse, but felt strangely comforted instead. This made no sense to her, but she accepted the comfort. She wished that she could tell Sandra about her real job, but she didn't dare. Perhaps Sandra wouldn't be shocked, but she would think it was self-destructive and insulting to women. Well, maybe it was. She never got any writing done while she was hooking. Somehow the idea of coming home after a day at Christine's and sitting down to write was impossible; her thoughts were clotted by the clamoring, demanding ghosts of the men she'd seen that day. She needed to make herself a nourishing meal and sit still and take care of herself, as her mother used to say. Working at Christine's was a time for making money and resting her brain, she told herself. Writing would come later.

She pictured herself in the future, so successful that she could talk about being a hooker without anyone minding. "I didn't do much writing then," she'd say to her circle of successful friends as they stood around smiling and holding their drinks. "I spent most of my time just trying to re-form my personality." And they'd all laugh at this adorable admission of her female vulnerability.

The only person she'd ever told was her friend from college, Babette. Babette, who was trying to be an actress, had a whole gaggle of friends from the restaurant where she worked who wore a lot of leather and went en masse to some S&M bar in the West Village on weekends. It didn't seem as though prostitution would faze Babette, but when Stephanie told her about her first experience three years earlier, she'd said, "Oh, Stephie! How could you do that to yourself? How could you?" Stephanie explained again and again that she didn't think it was damaging her self-respect, but Babette would not be mollified. Stephanie suspected that Babette's consternation had little to do with self-respect and a lot to do with Babette's discomfort at discovering that she was friends with a prostitute instead of a writer. However, Babette was a fragile person who had done too much cocaine, had a breakdown, cut her wrist—shallowly, but still—and now saw a therapist twice a week, so she thought it was best not to speak to her again about subsequent episodes.

She didn't see Bernard during the next three days, but she saw a variety of people unappealing enough to demolish her soothing daydream of happy prostitutes and fatherly johns. One, although he had made a point of showering and vigorously drying beforehand, dripped sweat off the tip of his nose and onto her face as ardently as he dripped his endearments, and seemed genuinely puzzled, even hurt, when she turned away from his kiss. Another, a huge, morose fellow with a gold Pisces chain on his fleshy chest, lay on his back and talked about how the most wonderful time in his life had been when he played football in high school; he was unable to figure out why everything had been so boring ever since. "I bet I know what you was like then," he said, rolling over. "You was one of them quiet types that never went out. And look at you now." There was no malice in his voice; it was a wonderless comment, which made its accuracy all the more depressing. Then there was the concave-chested little person who so offended her with the pre-session suggestion that she "suck his tits" that she involuntarily threw up her hands and said, "No. No. Just no," and walked out of the room and down the stairs, not caring whether or not Christine fired her, which she didn't. "I'll send one of the other girls up," she said to Stephanie as they huddled in the kitchen. "You've worked hard today and I can afford to lose that geek if he walks."

On the fourth day, when Bernard finally appeared, she fell into his arms. "I'm so glad to see you," she said, feeling his rather automatic placating response. She told him how terrible the last few days had been.

"This guy was there for half an hour droning about his stupid high school days, and how important he was, and how all the cute girls would go out with him. It was just dreadful." She noted Bernard's puzzled expression and laughed. "I guess it doesn't sound so bad, but it really was. For a while I was in his life, and his life was lousy."

He looked at her seriously. "You're right," he said. "You shouldn't be here. This is a bad place for you."

"I know. I'm going to quit next week."

"If you do, you must give me your phone number. I'd really like to keep in touch with you. It doesn't have to be any big deal. I just think you're an interesting girl."

She didn't see him before she quit, nor did he call her right away. When a week went by, she decided he'd changed his mind. She felt disappointed, but also relieved, and then stopped thinking about it. She eased back into her life slowly, first looking for another job and then trying to write every day.

Babette entered a period of energy and optimism and began asking her out to nightclubs again. Babette had a lot of friends in the club business, so they could unfailingly sail past the block-long lines of people vainly trying to catch some doorman's imperious eye. Babette, a tiny angular creature with long, slightly slanted eyes, looked annoyingly perfect in her silk Chinese jacket and black suede boots, her slim hip tilted one way, he little head the other. Stephanie always felt large and unraveled by comparison, as though her hat was wrong or her hem was falling out.

They could spend hours wandering through the dark rooms, holding their drinks and shouting comments at one another. Often they would meet friends of Babette's who would invite them into the bathroom for cocaine. Sometimes Babette would go off to dance and Stephanie would stand on the periphery of the dance floor, watching the dancers grinning and waving their arms in blind delight or staring severely at the floor as they thrashed their limbs. Lights flashed off and on, and the disc jockey spun one record after another in a pattern of controlled delirium. Stephanie would stroll through the club, watching the non-dancers blankly scrutinizing the dancers or standing in groups that were laughing with mysterious animation. After about fifteen minutes, she would be forced to face the fact that she was bored. Then she would remember what she was like before she came to New York and realize that this was what she had pictured: herself in a glamorous club full of laughing or morosely posing people. In frustration, she would decide that the reason it all seemed so dull was that she was seeing only the outermost layer of a complex society that spoke in ingenious and impenetrable signs to outsiders who, even if they were able to physically enter the club, were unable to enter the conversations that so amused everyone else. This was a discouraging idea, but it was better than thinking that the entire place was a nonsensical bore that people actually longed to belong in.

"Hi," said a man with a hideous hunk of hair. "I like your hat."

"Thank you."

"Would you like to dance?"

"No, thank you." She looked right at him when she said this, meaning to convey that she didn't consider him repulsive, but that she was deep in thought and couldn't dance.

It didn't work; he stared away with a ruffled air and then said, "Do you want to go to the Palladium?"

"No, thank you."

He looked at her with theatrical scorn and she noticed that he was actually very handsome. "Are you French?" he asked.

"No. Why do you ask? Do I sound French?"

"I don't know. You just look like you might be. Are you a dancer?"

"No. Why?"

"I don't know. You have to be something." He looked as if he was about to spit.

"What do you do?" she asked.

"I'm an architect. Do you want some coke?"

"No, thank you."

He looked at her as though she were completely mad and walked away. She quickly moved off the spot of this encounter toward a roomful of people in groups, determined to hear at least part of an interesting conversation. She was stopped by a man who wanted to know if she was Italian. She said no and escaped him. She was continuing toward a courtly group of large, aging transvestites who were the most welcoming and companionable bunch she'd seen all night when a very handsome black man took her elbow and said, "Bonsoir. Are you French?"

"No."

"Italian?"

"No."

His faced changed a shade. "What are you?"

"I'm from Illinois."

He dropped her elbow with unmistakable contempt and turned his back to her. That was the last straw. She walked out of the club and into the street, not even bothering to look for Babette.

She walked ten blocks in her high heels, and was almost home when she decided to stop at a neighborhood lesbian bar. It would be comfortable, she thought, to get drunk in the company of jovial women. And it was, until a pleasant conversation she thought she was having turned into a nasty argument, before she ever saw the turn, about whether or not bisexual women are lying cowards. Then she staggered home.

At twelve o'clock the next day she answered the phone, making her voice as feeble and throaty as possible, the better to parry Babette with a muddled excuse. She didn't recognize his voice right away, not even when he mentioned Christine's, and he was beginning to sound insulted when she finally said, "Oh, *hi*," her voice wobbling pleasingly (to her) and making her feel like a tousle-haired, mascara-smeared movie babe in a rumpled bed. He was in the neighborhood, and he wanted to meet her for lunch.

"Gosh, I'd like to, but I was out late last night, I'm still in bed and I look awful."

"Well, I'm disappointed, but maybe some other time."

"Well, maybe I could . . . where are you?"

Half an hour later she was sitting with him in an expensive eggs Benedict place, with waiters in black pants mincing about as a piped-in symphony identified this as a haven of Western civilization. "I tried to call you before, but you weren't at home and then I got incredibly busy. There's been a lot of fuss over a particular couple of blocks in the Village."

"I've heard," she said. "Actually, I wish they weren't doing that to the Village. It's going to be awfully sterile soon."

"That may be," he said easily. "But it would be sterile, not to say precious, if the old neighborhood were artificially maintained."

"Letting a place alone isn't the same thing as artificial maintenance. Anyway, this is artificially accelerated development." She argued with him happily, pointing out that he was contradicting an earlier-expressed belief that the government should manipulate the economy to protect the poor.

"Yes, I suppose you're right about that," he said after her short speech. His indifferent capitulation left her forceful argument charging foolishly toward a vanishing target, and she changed the subject, telling him about the previous night. He especially liked the drunken argument with the lesbian, and said "fabulous" three times.

Their eggs came in oblong dishes. The piped-in woodwinds sang stirringly of decency and order.

"What are you doing now that you've left Christine's?" he asked. "Are you working or writing?"

"Neither one, really." She thought: I'm trying to re-form my personality. "I'm looking for a job, probably some clerical thing. Maybe something part time."

"Have you considered something in an editorial capacity?"

"I tried that when I first came here and it didn't work out."

"Why not?"

She shrugged. "I guess I wasn't really interested enough." She thought of trying to explain herself further, but ate her eggs instead. She remembered herself newly arrived in New York, nervously planning her future. She saw the ensuing events as a series of comic-strip pictures separated by dark borders. This was especially true of her job search—there she was, the round-shouldered applicant before the monotonous, large-handed boss. She remembered her interview with the most respected editor of the most prestigious publishing house in town:

"Oh, yes, I remember Georgia Helman." The editor had rolled his eyes as he mentioned the woman who had referred Stephanie to him, a woman who had been his associate for two years. "A rather pathetic case. The only reason I hired her was as a favor to a personal friend. She was so messed up with drugs and men, you know. But about you." He looked at her as if she'd already been in his office several times. "If you really want to be a writer, then don't move to New York. You'll just wind up in some dank little dump in the East Village with bars on the windows, and oh, I don't know." He grimaced and flapped his hand with distaste.

She reminded him that she had already moved to the city and he said, "Well, in that case, maybe you should try *The New Yorker*. They generally hire only friends and family, but you have a certain, I don't know, fresh, insipid look they might like. I've gotten quite a few people in there. Would you like to have a drink tomorrow evening?"

She had to admit that a large part of the reason she was even trying to get a job was for the approval of people she'd known in Illinois, many of whom were living in New York and thought of her as a hopeless neurotic who couldn't do much of anything.

She thought of her last conversation with one of these people, a film production assistant on her lunch break. "Stephanie," she said, "you've simply got to cut your hair. I know it sounds superficial, but really, things like that matter. Editors are very busy people; they can only see you for twenty minutes, so they have to act on impressions, and that includes style. Long hair is college—ideals, finding yourself, and all that. Nobody here has long hair." She dug smartly into her pile of refried beans.

She thought of Jackson, an ex-lover whom she had especially wanted to impress, and was perversely glad that she never did get a professional position. She remembered what a curious relief it had been to take her first job in a whorehouse, where a real job didn't matter, where males and females performed the ancient, primal and wonderfully elementary dance of copulation, blandly, predictably and by appointment.

"Is something wrong?" asked Bernard.

"I was just thinking of someone." She hesitated. "Someone I knew in college. I had a pretty awful relationship with this person and I couldn't have sex for over a year afterward. The first time I fucked anybody else after him was my first trick in my first house."

"You're kidding!"

She laughed. "It's too corny, isn't it? Girl has heart broken by callous swine and turns to prostitution."

"Your life is very dramatic," he said pleasantly.

"It's not so dramatic. These things happen. I mean, I'm over it now."

Bernard walked her back to her building, but to her surprise he didn't want to come up to the apartment, even though she would have liked him to. In fact, they didn't fuck until the second time she had dinner with him. It was a calm, affectionate event ("I don't want to hurt you," he said, referring to his problematic size as he lay on top of her, gripping her firmly about the hips). The evening was marred only when he handed her a hundred dollars on his way out the door.

She stared at him, stricken. "I don't want that," she said. "That's not why I'm seeing you."

He looked embarrassed. "I know it's not why you're seeing me. It's not why I'm seeing you. But I think you should have it."

"I don't want it."

He sat on the bed. "Stephanie, it's very simple. I have a lot of money. You do not. You need money. I can give it to you. Please take it."

"You didn't give me money when we went out to dinner."

He groped for an explanation for this and gave up. "Well, the next time we go out to dinner, I'll give you money."

"I won't take it."

"If you don't, I'll just mail it to you."

Accepting the money became less troublesome than arguing. She stared at the cash sitting on her dresser after he left and thought: So now it is my real life. Then she got up and put it in her wallet.

The next few times she saw him, the cash factor didn't seem so bad. It even felt perversely glamorous; it made her think of Babette's friend Natalia, a dark, striking girl who was trying to be an actress. Babette was always telling Stephanie, with a certain awe, how Natalia collected men who bought her clothes and gave her money and drugs. If only Bernard would buy her a dress or something, perhaps it would seem less dubious, but she enjoyed his company, he was sexually pleasant, and she rather relished the novelty of the situation, much as he probably did. She told her friends that she was seeing a married man who "gave her money sometimes."

"Stephanie, that sounds really good for you," said Sandra. "Sometimes it's good to have somebody who will just come over to your house and be nice to you."

"I like that," said Bernard as he held her in his arms. "I'm a person who comes over to your house and is nice to you."

Besides, it had been three weeks since she'd quit Christine's, and she still hadn't found a job, so the money was useful to her. Sometimes it was a hundred, sometimes two or even three hundred, depending on nothing but his mood.

Her days began to slide together in a passive slur of afternoon movies, galleries and nightclubs. Babette would ask her if she'd started writing and she'd say that she was taking notes, which was true. She was content to drift, confident that her unconscious was unconsciously gathering information.

She was having coffee in Soho one afternoon when Jackson walked into the café. He had the same mincing, narrow walk, the same rigid pelvis, the same uptilted chin. He looked at her and she at him. She held her breath. He quickly examined her, from foot to eye, and sat down on the other side of the room without answering her nod.

She thought of something Babette had said when Stephanie had told her about her first hooking experience. "Oh, Stephie, don't you know this is exactly what Jackson said you'd do? How can you fall into that horrible idea he had of you?"

She had stiffly explained to Babette that this had nothing to do with Jackson, and she was sure that it didn't. But it made her feel bad to think of Jackson's reaction if he ever heard about it. The last time she'd seen him in New York, she had called him. He said they should meet for lunch, but lunch turned out to be a plastic glass of orange juice in a coffee shop while Jackson waited for his laundry to come out of a machine. He didn't have much time, he said. He was meeting his fiancée's parents at five. Their forty minutes of conversation were filled with pauses and downward looks. "People in New York are very busy," he said. "I divide my time sparingly between my work and my social life. I find myself associating primarily with other young professionals."

She told Bernard about seeing Jackson that night, as they sat in a loud bar having BLTs and drinks.

"It sounds romantic in a way," he said. "Silently passing each other in a crowded room."

"It was awful."

"What was so terrible about what happened between the two of you?"

She shrugged. "It's hard to describe. I guess it's basically that corny thing I talked about. I loved him, I trusted him too much and he turned out to be a dreadful person." She realized that Bernard was being distracted by a plump blonde with loopy earrings and white go-go boots. She paused until he turned toward her again. "But it was more complicated. He had a lot of power over me. He was bisexual—don't worry, I test negative—and he was seeing this guy André at the same time that he was seeing me. Sometimes he'd literally get up out of my bed and go be with André. Then he decided André and I should be friends and that we should all go out together."

"Why did you go along with this? Did you like it?"

"Yeah, that was part of it. I wanted to be open. I wanted to experience everything. And I loved Jackson, or thought I did. Eventually, I wound up in bed with both of them, and that's when it got ugly. I freaked out, Jackson decided I was boring and dropped me. That's it."

Bernard stared at her more intently than he ever had, with a deepening, almost gloating shade of something she couldn't read in his dark eyes. He clasped her hand under the table and held it tight.

"Even after he left Evanston, I felt as if the whole tone of my time there was set by my thing with him. Everybody there knew about the three of us. Everywhere I went I got these looks. Jackson had a lot of friends who weren't the most compassionate people in the world and . . . it was painful."

"But didn't such a complex liaison make you all the more mysterious and interesting to people?"

"I don't know. I didn't give a shit about being interesting and mysterious. I wanted him to love me."

For a second, he looked as though she had said something truly strange. Then his face smoothed over with fatherly tenderness. He stroked her cheek. "You really are a classic," he said. "You don't look it, but you are."

Three weeks after she'd started seeing Bernard, a month after she'd left Christine's, an unexpected thing happened. Someone from a magazine she had interviewed with when she had come to New York three years before called her about a position as an editorial assistant. They had found her résumé and clips from the Evanston college paper in an old file and wanted to know if she was available. It was an architectural journal—not a subject she cared much about, but she remembered the magazine as being well written and beautifully designed. Besides, she was becoming desperate for a job, so she had the interview and was hired two days later.

Babette and Sandra seemed to think that it was the most wonderful thing in the world. (Now Sandra no longer had to stretch Stephanie's connection with the *Voice,* and could introduce her as "in editorial.") Stephanie wasn't sure that it would in fact be a lot better than working at Christine's; she no longer cared about being a "young professional" for Jackson's sake.

Meanwhile, her odd relationship with Bernard was beginning to trouble her. Their conversation, although they spoke of many things, seemed mostly polite and for the benefit of fantasies they had about each other. Sexually, they seemed to be on the same level. She couldn't tell if this was disappointing to him or not. And the money issue was beginning to disturb her again, now that she was working for the magazine. He's not someone who comes to my house and is nice to me, she thought as she lay alone in bed. He's someone who pays me to fuck him. She had an image of herself, sprawled half on and half off a bed at Christine's, her upside-down head patiently looking back at her from the mirror as some galoot humped her. This vision blended discordantly with the idea of herself at her desk at the magazine and she was unable to separate them.

Despite this ambiguity, she was curiously reluctant to drop the affair. He only saw her once or twice a week, he was not demanding, he liked her favorite authors and was somehow very reassuring. Reassuring of what, she didn't know, but it was connected to her old feeling that he thought of her as a representative of the exciting avant-garde—although it also seemed that if he had any brains at all, he would've realized by now that she was just a bewildered human.

"I think I know why you go to places like Christine's," she said.

"I'm all ears."

"One of the times I was there, I was watching this girl called Marissa, a skinny, not very attractive girl with blank brown eyes. It was almost the end of the night and she was squatting on the floor with her skirt hiked up to her waist, counting her money with a little furry-animal look of concentration, and I thought about how she must look to someone like you, despite her nasty personality — like this cute little beast who can be swept up and fondled and experienced and then put down."

"That's fabulous." He looked deeply entertained. "You have such a wonderful way of expressing things."

She thought: If he says "fabulous" one more time tonight, I may punch him in the nose.

It was a cool autumn evening. Clawlike leaves smelling of ashes rasped and scuttled across the pavement as they walked to her apartment.

They were silent and she felt uncomfortable about it. They were returning from a dinner that should've been nice but wasn't. Bernard had been distracted and (she felt) bored by her. He had flirted subtly with their waitress, which she'd observed with a detached sense of disappointment, a cold and lifeless form of jealousy. As they mounted the stairs, she felt they were heading toward a destination simply because it was more trouble than it was worth to avoid it.

Once inside the warm apartment, though, she felt better about him, and she sensed a similar change in his mood. They lay snuggled on her bed and told short stories about their lives. He mentioned a girl he'd had a particular passion for in college, a headstrong dancer with long red hair, and told how he had finally seduced her one night after a party. "It was one of the most exciting experiences of my life. At the last moment she panicked and said, 'No, let me just take you in my mouth.'"

"Why didn't she want to screw?"

"Because she felt too vulnerable and didn't want me to enter her."

"What happened?"

"Well, I fucked her." Pause. "And that was the beginning of a long and intense relationship."

"Did you ever consider marrying her?"

What a silly idea, said his face. "No, no. I wasn't thinking about that then."

"Did you ever feel a passion like that for your wife?"

"No, I really didn't. She was by far the most beautiful of all the women I'd been with, but I wasn't nearly as attracted to her as I had been to the others." He touched her nose. "You're really concerned about that, aren't you?"

They kissed and petted, and her absurd bed creaked. Then they separated and talked again. She told him about the time her sister's boyfriend had tried to seduce her in the middle of their breakup.

"What happened?" He smiled.

"Nothing. I didn't want to. I mean, I wasn't attracted to him and he was obviously doing it out of hostility to my sister."

"Oh, no. That probably had nothing to do with it."

"Well, maybe not. I think part of it was that he was intrigued by me as a variation of her."

"Exactly!" He said this with great emphasis, as though she'd hit upon something important. "I almost seduced my wife's sister the first time we separated, but we both balked at the last minute, mostly her. We were at the kitchen table, drinking gin." He smiled. "Of course your sister's boyfriend wanted you. One wants them all."

She began to talk about an old lover of hers who reminded her of Bernard, but as she talked she kept imagining Bernard on a clean tiled kitchen floor, humping his blond wife's blond sister. It reminded her of the stories in *The New Yorker* about decent professional people having extramarital affairs. The more she contemplated this picture, the more difficult it was to imagine sex with this man . . . this customer. She had a quick feeling of sympathy for his wife, lying in her single bed, in her separate room, next to the room of a man who wanted them all. She started to feel something like guilt, and to forestall it, she began to kiss him. The bed creaked and he parted her legs.

From that moment on, the same sense of disaffection that she'd felt in the restaurant overtook her. Afterward, they spoke some more, but the conversation didn't work. They even had a strangely snide argument about whether or not Nabokov was a good writer. In the frequent silences, she felt that he sensed her sudden disapproval of him. She was a little sorry, because she liked him, but at the same time she was relieved when he got up to go. When he said "Take good care of yourself," she knew that she wouldn't hear from him again.

It wasn't until half an hour after he'd left that she realized that for the first time he hadn't left her any money. This had an entirely unexpected effect on her; she sat on her bed and cried.

She couldn't have said what she was crying about. Christine's, Brett, Jackson, her first miserable, lonely year in New York and Bernard the lawyer all seemed to have something to do with it, although she couldn't tell if she was just pulling anything available into her sadness. She cried until she was sure she was absolutely finished. Then she got up, put on her shoes and went out for a walk.

It was a beautiful Halloweenlike night, and there were exuberant people on the streets. She walked happily, admiring faces and haircuts. She looked at people, dogs, cars and buildings, and everything pleased her. She stopped at a Korean grocery store and looked at the fruit. She was struck by how neat and beautiful it was in its organized, traditional piles. She thought of herself coming here every week and buying fruit, vegetables, bread, cereal and milk, and it seemed like a wonderful idea. She bought herself an apple, and walked home eating it.

Secretary

THE TYPING AND secretarial class was held in a little basement room in the Business Building of the local community college. The teacher was an old lady with hair that floated in vague clouds around her temples and Kleenex stuck up the sleeve of her dress for some future, probably nasal purpose. She held a stopwatch in one old hand and tilted her hip as she watched us all with severe, imperial eyes, not caring that her stomach hung out. The girl in front of me had short, clenched blond curls sitting on her thin shoulders. Lone strands would stick straight out from her head in cold, dry weather.

It was a two-hour class with a ten-minute break. Everybody would go out in the hall during the break to get coffee or candy from the machines. The girls would stand in groups and talk, and the two male typists would walk slowly up and down the corridor with round shoulders, holding their Styrofoam cups and looking into the bright slits of light in the business class doors as they passed by.

I would go to the big picture window that looked out onto the parking lot and stare at the streetlights shining on the hoods of the cars.

After class, I'd come home and put my books on the dining room table among the leftover dinner things: balled-up napkins, glasses of water, a dish of green beans sitting on a pot holder. My father's plate would always be there, with gnawed bones and hot pepper on it. He would be in the living room in his pajama top with a dish of ice cream in his lap and his hair on end. "How many words a minute did you type tonight?" he'd ask.

It wasn't an unreasonable question, but the predictable and agitated delivery of it was annoying. It reflected his way of hoarding silly details and his obsessive fear I would meet my sister's fate. She'd had a job at a home for retarded people for the past eight years. She wore jeans and a long army coat to work every day. When she came home, she went up to her room and lay in bed. Every now and then she would come down and joke around or watch TV, but not much.

Mother would drive me around to look for jobs. First we would go through ads in the paper, drawing black circles, marking X's. The defaced newspaper sat on the dining room table in a gray fold and we argued.

"I'm not friendly and I'm not personable. I'm not going to answer an ad for somebody like that. It would be stupid."

"You can be friendly. And you are personable when you aren't busy putting yourself down."

"I'm not putting myself down. You just want to think that I am so you can have something to talk about."

"You're backing yourself into a corner, Debby."

"Oh, shit." I picked up a candy wrapper and began pinching it together in an ugly way. My hands were red and rough. It didn't matter how much lotion I used.

"Come on, we're getting started on the wrong foot."

"Shut up."

My mother crossed her legs. "Well," she said. She picked up the "Living" section of the paper and cracked it into position. She tilted her head back and dropped her eyelids. Her upper lip became hostile as she read. She picked up her green teacup and drank.

"I'm dependable. I could answer an ad for somebody dependable."

"You are that."

We wound up in the car. My toes swelled in my high heels. My mother and I both used the flowered box of Kleenex on the dashboard and stuck the used tissue in a brown bag that sat near the hump in the middle of the car. There was a lot of traffic in both lanes. We drove past the Amy Joy doughnut shop. They still hadn't put the letter Y back on the Amy sign.

Our first stop was Wonderland. There was a job in the clerical department of Sears. The man there had a long disapproving nose, and he held his hands stiffly curled in the middle of his desk. He mainly looked at his hands. He said he would call me, but I knew he wouldn't.

On the way back to the parking lot, we passed a pet store. There were only hamsters, fish and exhausted yellow birds. We stopped and looked at slivers of fish swarming in their tank of thick green water. I had come to this pet store when I was ten years old. The mall had just opened and we had all come out to walk through it. My sister, Donna, had wanted to go into the pet store. It was very warm and damp in the store, and smelled like fur and hamster. When we walked out, it seemed cold. I said I was cold and Donna took off her white leatherette jacket and put it around my shoulders, letting one hand sit on my left shoulder for a minute. She had never touched me like that before and she hasn't since.

The next place was a tax information office in a slab of building with green trim. They gave me an intelligence test that was mostly spelling and "What's wrong with this sentence?" The woman came out of her office holding my test and smiling. "You scored higher than anyone else I've interviewed," she said. "You're really overqualified for this job. There's no challenge. You'd be bored to death."

"I want to be bored," I said.

She laughed. "Oh, I don't think that's true."

We had a nice talk about what people want out of their jobs and then I left.

"Well, I hope you weren't surprised that you had the highest score," said my mother.

We went to the French bakery on Eight-Mile Road and got cookies called elephant ears. We ate them out of a bag as we drove. I felt so comfortable, I could have driven around in the car all day.

Then we went to a lawyer's office on Telegraph Road. It was a receding building made of orange brick. There were no other houses or stores around it, just a parking lot and some taut fir trees that looked like they had been brushed. My mother waited for me in the car. She smiled, took out a crossword puzzle and focused her eyes on it, the smile still gripping her face.

The lawyer was a short man with dark, shiny eyes and dense immobile shoulders. He took my hand with an indifferent aggressive snatch. It felt like he could have put his hand through my rib cage, grabbed my heart, squeezed it a little to see how it felt, then let go. "Come into my office," he said.

We sat down and he fixed his eyes on me. "It's not much of a job," he said. "I have a paralegal who does research and leg-work, and the proofreading gets done at an agency. All I need is a presentable typist who can get to work on time and answer the phone."

"I can do that," I said.

"It's very dull work," he said.

"I like dull work."

He stared at me, his eyes becoming hooded in thought. "There's something about you," he said. "You're closed up, you're tight. You're like a wall."

"I know."

My answer surprised him and his eyes lost their hoods. He tilted his head back and looked at me, his shiny eyes bared again. "Do you ever loosen up?"

The corners of my mouth jerked, smilelike. "I don't know." My palms sweated.

His secretary, who was leaving, called me the next day and said that he wanted to hire me. Her voice was serene, flat and utterly devoid of inflection.

"That typing course really paid off," said my father. "You made a good investment." He wandered in and out of the dining room in pleased agitation, holding his glass of beer. "A law office could be a fascinating place." He arched his chin and scratched his throat.

Donna even came downstairs and made popcorn and put it in a big yellow bowl on the table for everybody to eat. She ate lazily, her large hand dawdling in the bowl. "It could be okay. Interesting people could come in. Even though that lawyer's probably an asshole."

My mother sat quietly, pleased with her role in the job-finding project, pinching clusters of popcorn in her fingers and popping them into her mouth.

That night I put my new work clothes on a chair and looked at them. A brown skirt, a beige blouse. I was attracted to the bland ugliness, but I didn't know how long that would last. I looked at their gray shapes in the night-light and then rolled over toward the dark corner of my bed.

My family's enthusiasm made me feel sarcastic about the job — about any effort to do anything, in fact. In light of their enthusiasm, the only intelligent course of action seemed to be immobility and rudeness. But in the morning, as I ate my poached eggs and toast, I couldn't help but feel curious and excited. The feeling grew as I rode in the car with my mother to the receding orange building. I felt like I was accomplishing something. I wanted to do well. When we drove past the Amy Joy doughnut shop, I saw, through a wall of glass, expectant construction workers in heavy boots and jackets sitting on vinyl swivel seats, waiting for coffee and bags of doughnuts. I had sentimental thoughts about workers and the decency of unthinking toil. I was pleased to be like them, insofar as I was. I returned my mother's smile when I got out of the car and said "thanks" when she said "good luck."

"Well, here you are," said the lawyer. He clapped his short, hard-packed little hands together and made a loud noise. "On time. Good morning!"

He began training me then and continued to do so all week. No interesting people came into the office. Very few people came into the office at all. The first week there were three. One was a nervous middle-aged woman who had an uneven haircut and was wearing lavender rubber children's boots. She sat on the edge of the waiting room chair with her rubber boots together, rearranging the things in her purse. Another was a fat woman in a bright, baglike dress who had yellow in the whites of her wild little eyes, and who carried her purse like a weapon. The last was a man who sat desperately turning his head as if he wanted to disconnect it from his body. I could hear him raising his voice inside the lawyer's office. When he left, the lawyer came out and said, "He is completely crazy," and told me to type him a bill for five hundred dollars.

Everyone who sat in the waiting room looked random and

unwelcome. They all fidgeted. The elegant old armchairs and puffy upholstered couch were themselves disoriented in the stiff modernity of the waiting room. My heavy oak desk was an idiot standing against a wall covered with beige plaster. The brooding plants before me gave the appearance of weighing a lot for plants, even though one of them was a slight, frondy thing.

I was surprised that a person like the lawyer, who seemed to be mentally organized and evenly distributed, would have such an office. But I was comfortable in it. Its jumbled nature was like a nest of available rags gathered tightly together for warmth. My first two weeks were serene. I enjoyed the dullness of days, the repetition of motions, the terms, polite interactions between the lawyer and me. I enjoyed feeling him impose his brainlessly confident sense of existence on me. He would say, "Type this letter," and my sensibility would contract until the abstractions of achievement and production found expression in the typing of the letter. I was useful.

My mother picked me up every day. We would usually stop at the A&P before we went home to get a loaf of white French bread, beer and kielbasa sausage for my father. When we got home I would go upstairs to my room, take off my shirt and blouse, and throw them on the floor. I would get into my bed of jumbled blankets in my underwear and panty hose and listen to my father yelling at my mother until I fell asleep. I woke up when Donna pounded on my door and yelled, "Dinner!"

I would go down with her then and sit at the table. We would all watch the news on TV as we ate. My mother would have a shrunken, abstracted look on her face. My father would hunch over his plate like an animal at its dish.

After dinner, I would go upstairs and listen to records and write in my diary or play Parcheesi with Donna until it was time to get ready for bed. I'd go to sleep at night looking at the skirt and blouse I would wear the next day. I'd wake up looking at my ceramic weather poodle, which was supposed to turn pink, blue or green, depending on the weather, but had only turned gray and stayed gray. I would hear my father in the bathroom, the tumble of radio patter, the water, the clink of a glass being set down, the creak and click as he closed the medicine cabinet. Donna would be standing outside my door, waiting for him to finish, muttering "shit" or something.

Looking back on it, I don't know why that time was such a contented one, but it was.

The first day of the third week, the lawyer came out of his office, stiffer than usual, his eyes lit up in a peculiar, stalking way. He was carrying one of my letters. He put it on my desk, right in front of me. "Look at it," he said. I did.

"Do you see that?"

"What?" I asked.

"This letter has three typing errors in it, one of which is, I think, a spelling error."

"I'm sorry."

"This isn't the first time either. There have been others that I let go because it was your first few weeks. But this can't go on. Do you know what this makes me look like to the people who receive these letters?"

I looked at him, mortified. There had been a catastrophe hidden in the folds of my contentment for two weeks and he hadn't even told me. It seemed unfair, although when I thought about it I could understand his reluctance, maybe even embarrassment, to draw my attention to something so stupidly unpleasant.

"Type it again."

I did, but I was so badly shaken that I made even more mistakes. "You are wasting my time," he said, and handed it to me once again. I typed it correctly the third time, but he sulked in his office for the rest of the day.

This kind of thing kept occurring all week. Each time, the lawyer's irritation and disbelief mounted. In addition, I sensed something else growing in him, an intimate tendril creeping from one of his darker areas, nursed on the feeling that he had discovered something about me.

I was very depressed about the situation. When I went home in the evening I couldn't take a nap. I lay there looking at the gray weather poodle and fantasized about having a conversation with

the lawyer that would clear up everything, explain to him that I
was really trying to do my best. He seemed to think that I was
making the mistakes on purpose.

At the end of the week he began complaining about the way I
answered the phone. "You're like a machine," he said. "You sound
like you're in the Twilight Zone. You don't think when you respond to people."

When he asked me to come into his office at the end of the day, I
thought he was going to fire me. The idea was a relief, but a numb-
ing one. I sat down and he fixed me with a look that was speculative
but benign, for him. He leaned back in his chair in a comfortable
way, one hand dangling sideways from his wrist. To my surprise,
he began talking to me about my problems, as he saw them.

"I sense that you are a very nice but complex person, with wild
mood swings that you keep hidden. You just shut up the house and
act like there's nobody home."

"That's true," I said. "I do that."

"Well, why? Why don't you open up a little bit? It would probably help your typing."

It was really not any of his business, I thought.

"You should try to talk more. I know I'm your employer and
we have a prescribed relationship, but you should feel free to discuss your problems with me."

The idea of discussing my problems with him was preposterous. "It's hard to think of having that kind of discussion with you,"
I said. I hesitated. "You have a strong personality and . . . when
I encounter a personality like that, I tend to step back because I
don't know how to deal with it."

He was clearly pleased with this response, but he said, "You
shouldn't be so shy."

When I thought about this conversation later, it seemed, on
the one hand, that this lawyer was just an asshole. On the other,
his comments were weirdly moving, and had the effect of making
me feel horribly sensitive. No one had ever made such personal
comments to me before.

The next day I made another mistake. The intimacy of the

previous day seemed to make the mistake even more repulsive to him because he got madder than usual. I wanted him to fire me. I would have suggested it, but I was struck silent. I sat and stared at the letter while he yelled. "What's wrong with you!"

"I'm sorry," I said.

He stood quietly for a moment. Then he said, "Come into my office. And bring that letter."

I followed him into his office.

"Put that letter on my desk," he said.

I did.

"Now bend over so that you are looking directly at it. Put your elbows on the desk and your face very close to the letter."

Shaken and puzzled, I did what he said.

"Now read the letter to yourself. Keep reading it over and over again."

I read: "Dear Mr. Garvy: I am very grateful to you for referring . . ." He began spanking me as I said "referring." The funny thing was, I wasn't even surprised. I actually kept reading the letter, although my understanding of it was not very clear. I began crying on it, which blurred the ink. The word "humiliation" came into my mind with such force that it effectively blocked out all other words. Further, I felt that the concept it stood for had actually been a major force in my life for quite a while.

He spanked me for about ten minutes, I think. I read the letter only about five times, partly because it rapidly became too wet to be legible. When he stopped he said, "Now straighten up and go type it again."

I went to my desk. He closed the office door behind him. I sat down, blew my nose and wiped my face. I stared into space for several minutes, every now and then dwelling on the tingling sensation in my buttocks. I typed the letter again and took it into his office. He didn't look up as I put it on his desk.

I went back out and sat, planning to sink into a stupor of some sort. But a client came in, so I couldn't. I had to buzz the lawyer and tell him the client had arrived. "Tell him to wait," he said curtly.

When I told the client to wait, he came up to my desk and

began to talk to me. "I've been here twice before," he said. "Do you recognize me?"

"Yes," I said. "Of course." He was a small, tight-looking middle-aged man with agitated little hands and a pale scar running over his lip and down his chin. The scar didn't make him look tough; he was too anxious to look tough.

"I never thought anything like this would ever happen to me," he said. "I never thought I'd be in a lawyer's office even once, and I've been here three times now. And absolutely nothing's been accomplished. I've always hated lawyers." He looked as though he expected me to take offense.

"A lot of people do," I said.

"It was either that or I would've shot those miserable blankety-blanks next door and I'd have to get a lawyer to defend me anyway. You know the story?"

I did. He was suing his neighbors because they had a dog that "barked all goddamn day." I listened to him talk. It surprised me how this short conversation quickly restored my sensibility. Everything seemed perfectly normal by the time the lawyer came out of his office to greet the client. I noticed he had my letter in one hand. Just before he turned to lead the client away, he handed it to me, smiling. "Good letter," he said.

When I went home that night, everything was the same. My life had not been disarranged by the event except for a slight increase in the distance between me and my family. My behind was not even red when I looked at it in the bathroom mirror.

But when I got into bed and thought about the thing, I got excited. I was more excited, in fact, than I had ever been in my life. That didn't surprise me, either. I felt a numbness; I felt that I could never have a normal conversation with anyone again. I masturbated slowly, to put off the climax as long as I could. But there was no climax, even though I tried for a long time. Then I couldn't sleep.

It happened twice more in the next week and a half. The following week, when I made a typing mistake, he didn't spank me. Instead, he told me to bend over his desk, look at the typing mistake and repeat "I am stupid" for several minutes.

Our relationship didn't change otherwise. He was still brisk and friendly in the morning. And, because he seemed so sure of himself, I could not help but react to him as if he were still the same domineering but affable boss. He did not, however, ever invite me to discuss my problems with him again.

I began to have recurring dreams about him. In one, the most frequent, I walked with him in a field of big bright red poppies. The day was brilliant and warm. We were smiling at each other, and there was a tremendous sense of release and goodwill between us. He looked at me and said, "I understand you now, Debby." Then we held hands.

There was one time I felt disturbed about what was happening at the office. It was just before dinner, and my father was upset about something that had happened to him at work. I could hear him yelling in the living room while my mother tried to comfort him. He yelled, "I'd rather work in a circus! In one of those things where you put your head through a hole and people pay to throw garbage at you!"

"No circus has that anymore," said my mother. "Stop it, Shep."

By the time I went down to eat dinner, everything was as usual. I looked at my father and felt a sickening sensation of love nailed to contempt and panic.

The last time I made a typing error and the lawyer summoned me to his office, two unusual things occurred. The first was that after he finished spanking me he told me to pull up my skirt. Fear hooked my stomach and pulled it toward my chest. I turned my head and tried to look at him.

"You're not worried that I'm going to rape you, are you?" he said. "Don't. I'm not interested in that, not in the least. Pull up your skirt.

I turned my head away from him. I thought, I don't have to do this. I can stop right now. I can straighten up and walk out. But I didn't. I pulled up my skirt.

"Pull down your panty hose and underwear."

A finger of nausea poked my stomach.

"I told you I'm not going to fuck you. Do what I say."

The skin on my face and throat was hot, but my fingertips were cold on my legs as I pulled down my underwear and pantyhose. The letter before me became distorted beyond recognition. I thought I might faint or vomit, but I didn't. I was held up by a feeling of dizzying suspension, like the one I have in dreams where I can fly, but only if I get into some weird position.

At first he didn't seem to be doing anything. Then I became aware of a small frenzy of expended energy behind me. I had an impression of a vicious little animal frantically burrowing dirt with its tiny claws and teeth. My hips were sprayed with hot sticky muck.

"Go clean yourself off," he said. "And do that letter again."

I stood slowly, and felt my skirt fall over the sticky gunk. He briskly swung open the door and I left the room, not even pulling up my panty hose and underwear, since I was going to use the bathroom anyway. He closed the door behind me, and the second unusual thing occurred. Susan, the paralegal, was standing in the waiting room with a funny look on her face. She was a blonde who wore short, fuzzy sweaters, and fake gold jewelry around her neck. At her friendliest, she had a whining, abrasive quality that clung to her voice. Now, she could barely say hello. Her stupidly full lips were parted speculatively.

"Hi," I said. "Just a minute." She noted the awkwardness of my walk, because of the lowered panty hose.

I got to the bathroom and wiped myself off. I didn't feel embarrassed. I felt mechanical. I wanted to get that dumb paralegal out of the office so I could come back to the bathroom and masturbate.

Susan completed her errand and left. I masturbated. I retyped the letter. The lawyer sat in his office all day.

When my mother picked me up that afternoon, she asked me if I was all right.

"Why do you ask?"

"I don't know. You look a little strange."

"I'm as all right as I ever am."

"That doesn't sound good, honey."

I didn't answer. My mother moved her hands up and down the steering wheel, squeezing it anxiously.

"Maybe you'd like to stop by the French bakery and get some elephant ears," she said.

"I don't want any elephant ears." My voice was unexpectedly nasty. It almost made me cry.

"All right," said my mother.

When I lay on my bed to take my nap, my body felt dense and heavy, as though it would be very hard to move again, which was just as well, since I didn't feel like moving. When Donna banged on my door and yelled "Dinner!" I didn't answer. She put her head in and asked if I was asleep, and I told her I didn't feel like eating. I felt so inert, I thought I'd go to sleep, but I couldn't. I lay awake through the sounds of argument and TV and everybody going to the bathroom. Bedtime came, drawers rasped open and shut, doors slammed, my father eased into sleep with radio mumble. The orange digits on my clock said 1:30. I thought: I should get out of this panty hose and slip. I sat up and looked out into the gray, cold street. The shrubbery on the lawn across the street looked frozen and miserable. I thought about the period of time a year before when I couldn't sleep because I kept thinking that someone was going to break into the house and kill everybody. Eventually that fear went away and I went back to sleeping again. I lay back down without taking off my clothes, and pulled a light blanket tightly around me. Sooner or later, I thought, I would sleep. I would just have to wait.

But I didn't sleep, although I became mentally incoherent for long, ugly stretches of time. Hours went by; the room turned gray. I heard the morning noises: the toilet, the coughing, Donna's hostile muttering. Often, in the past, I had woken early and lain in bed listening to my family clumsily trying to organize itself for the day. Often as not, their sounds made me feel irrational loathing. This morning, I felt despair and a longing for them, and a sureness that we would never be close as long as I lived. My nasal passages became active with tears that didn't reach my eyes.

My mother knocked on the door. "Honey, aren't you going to be late?"

"I'm not going to work. I feel sick. I'll call in."

"I'll do it for you, just stay in bed."

"No, I'm going to call. It has to be me."

I didn't call in. The lawyer didn't call the house. I didn't go in or call the next day or the day after that. The lawyer still didn't call. I was slightly hurt by his absent phone call, but my relief was far greater than my hurt.

After I'd stayed home for four days, my father asked if I wasn't worried about taking so much time off. I told him I'd quit, in front of Donna and my mother. He was dumbfounded.

"That wasn't very smart," he said. "What are you going to do now?"

"I don't care," I said. "That lawyer was an asshole." To everyone's discomfort, I began to cry. I left the room, and they all watched me stomp up the stairs.

The next day at dinner my father said, "Don't get discouraged because your first job didn't work out. There're plenty of other places out there."

"I don't want to think about another job right now."

There was a disgruntlement all around the table. "Come on now, Debby, you don't want to throw away everything you worked for in that typing course," said my father.

"I don't blame her," said Donna. "I'm sick of working for assholes."

"Oh, shit," said my father. "If I had quit every job I've had on those grounds, you would've all starved. Maybe that's what I should've done."

"What happened, Debby?" said my mother.

I said, "I don't want to talk about it," and I left the room again.

After that they may have sensed, with their intuition for the miserable, that something hideous had happened. Because they left the subject alone.

I received my last paycheck from the lawyer in the mail. It came with a letter folded around it. It said, "I am so sorry for what happened between us. I have realized what a terrible mistake I made with you. I can only hope that you will understand, and that you will not worsen an already unfortunate situation by discussing it with others. All the best." As a P.S. he assured me that I could count on him for excellent references. He enclosed a check for three hundred and eighty dollars, a little over two hundred dollars more than he owed me.

It occurred to me to tear up the check, or mail it back to the lawyer. But I didn't do that. Two hundred dollars was worth more then than it is now. Together with the money I had in the bank, it was enough to put a down payment on an apartment and still have some left over. I went upstairs and wrote "380" on the deposit side of my checking account. I didn't feel like a whore or anything. I felt I was doing the right thing. I looked at the total figure of my balance with satisfaction. Then I went downstairs and asked my mother if she wanted to go get some elephant ears.

For the next two weeks, I forgot about the idea of a job and moving out of my parents' house. I slept through all the morning noise until noon. I got up and ate cold cereal and ran the dishwasher. I watched the gray march of old sitcoms on TV. I worked on crossword puzzles. I lay on my bed in a tangle of quilt and fuzzy blanket and masturbated two, three, four times in a row, always thinking about the thing.

I was still in this phase when my father stuck the newspaper under my nose and said, "Did you see what your old boss is doing?" There was a small article on the upcoming mayoral elections in Westland. He was running for mayor. I took the paper from my father's offering hands. For the first time, I felt an uncomplicated disgust for the lawyer. Westland was nothing but malls and doughnut stands and a big ugly theater with an artificial volcano in the front of it. What kind of idiot would want to be mayor of Westland? Again, I left the room.

I got the phone call the next week. It was a man's voice, a soft, probing, condoling voice. "Miss Roe?" he said. "I hope you'll forgive this unexpected call. I'm Mark Charming of *Detroit Magazine.*"

I didn't say anything. The voice continued more uncertainly. "Are you free to talk, Miss Roe?"

There was no one in the kitchen, and my mother was running the vacuum in the next room. "Talk about what?" I said.

"Your previous employer." The voice became slightly harsh as he said these words, and then hurriedly rushed back to condolence. "Please don't be startled or upset. I know this could be a disturbing phone call for you, and it must certainly seem intrusive." He paused so I could laugh or something. I didn't, and his voice became more cautious. "The thing is, we're doing a story on your ex-employer in the context of his running for mayor. To put it mildly, we think he has no business running for public office. We think he would be very bad for the whole Detroit area. He has an awful reputation, Miss Roe—which may not surprise you." There was another careful pause that I did not fill.

"Miss Roe, are you still with me?"

"Yes."

"What all this is leading up to is that we have reason to believe that you could reveal information about your ex-employer that would be damaging to him. This information would never be connected to your name. We would use a pseudonym. Your privacy would be protected completely."

The vacuum cleaner shut off, and silence encircled me. My throat constricted.

"Do you want time to think about it, Miss Roe?"

"I can't talk now," I said, and hung up.

I couldn't go through the living room without my mother asking me who had been on the phone, so I went downstairs to the basement. I sat on the mildewed couch and curled up, unmindful of centipedes. I rested my chin on my knee and stared at the boxes of my father's old paperbacks and the jumble of plastic Barbie-doll cases full of Barbie equipment that Donna and I used to play with on the front porch. A stiff white foot and calf stuck out of a sky-blue case, helpless and pitifully rigid.

For some reason, I remembered the time, a few years before, when my mother had taken me to see a psychiatrist. One of the more obvious questions he had asked me was, "Debby, do you ever have the sensation of being outside yourself, almost as if you can actually watch yourself from another place?" I hadn't at the time, but I did now. And it wasn't such a bad feeling at all.

Other Factors

CONSTANCE WAS DISCONCERTED by her meeting with Franklin in the East Village, partly because two years before he'd spent exactly one week ardently trying to seduce her, and then had abruptly dropped her to get married to a hitherto undisclosed fiancée. But there were other factors. "Constance!" he yelled. "God, it's great to see you! You're looking good! In fact, you're looking beautiful!"

The last time she had seen him had been at his wedding party; he'd been lip-synching to Grand Master Flash and doing an arm-flapping dance that threatened to tear the armpits out of his rented tux. Since then his nose seemed to have grown larger and lumpier, his face broader and his eyes more prone to wander frantically over the head of whomever he was talking to. But he still had his kind demeanor and his air that whatever he was talking about and whoever he was talking to were both equally and desperately important. She remembered something he had said to her sometime before: "Don't worry, Connie. In fifteen years, I'll be doing my retrospective at the Whitney and you'll be publishing regularly in *The New Yorker.*" He paused. "But by then we'll be ugly."

She smiled at him on the crowded street and they yelled cheerfully back and forth. He was busy, very busy, writing art criticism for three publications, teaching part-time and painting. She was doing free-lance journalism, and was currently huddled in a cranny of stability as a part-time editor for a slick literary quarterly. They linked arms and went for coffee.

"God," he said, hunching over his tiny brown cup of espresso, "it's good to see a new face. For weeks I've seen nobody but friends of Emily's who've come in from Dallas—these really incredible women who're all painters, all in their forties, incredibly intelligent and—would you believe it?—all *single*. They're great, but I feel like I have to constantly be telling them how attractive and talented they are—and they are attractive! They're incredibly attractive!— because they're in their forties, and they're not married, and they're not successful."

"What makes you think you always have to tell them how great they are?"

"You just do. It's obvious." He lifted the little brown cup in his big hands and delicately inserted the tip of his tongue, put it down and played with his napkin.

"You wouldn't have to tell me that if I was forty."

He didn't respond to this, but stared fixedly into a corner for several seconds and then said, "So, whose heart are you laying waste to now?"

"You mean who's trashing me these days? I'm not so extreme anymore, Franklin."

Franklin smiled in the sly, flatly pleased way he contrived when she simultaneously ridiculed and accepted his flattery.

"Actually, I have a girlfriend." She picked up her croissant as if she were going to bat her eyelashes from behind it. "We've been together for a year and a half. We live together."

"Connie, that's great. That's really super. Is this a new predilection?"

"No, it's always been there. This is just more serious than usual."

"You know, if she were a boy, I think I'd be jealous. Where'd you meet her?"

They burrowed into a conversation that skimmed over the present, then tunneled back through the five years since they'd met in a proofreading booth, where exhausted, languid Connie would sleep on the floor beneath her desk, using Franklin's balled-up sweater as a pillow. They had nested in that booth every weekend for months, surrounded by literary supplements, plastic take-out containers, boxes of cookies and notebooks in which they furiously scribbled between jobs. It was where they had staged their lengthy, horribly detailed conferences about their sexual relationships. "The nightmare of the two thousand and one dates," Franklin called it—or maybe she'd invented the nightmare part, she couldn't remember. The tunnel deepened as they entered a thickly populated realm of old friends, acquaintances, scandals and memories that appeared like frail, large-eyed animals that paused to look at them, then blinked and ran away.

Connie stopped a moment as Franklin talked and put her head up to survey the outside world; the dark café was crowded with young people in big jackets and neat, mincing shoes. A grotesquely beautiful girl in pink leather seemed to be staring at them. Did they look like pathetic aging hipsters? Was her hair wrong? Was their conversation too loud? Franklin was talking very loudly about a nasty exchange he'd had with another critic at some club. She winced, then took shelter in his apparently inexhaustible confidence and burrowed again. Then other factors raised their heads.

"You know, I had dinner with Alice and Roger last week," he said, tearing a bite out of his little sponge cake.

Constance halted in her burrowing. "I thought you didn't see them anymore."

"What? Why?"

"What about that big fight you had with Roger?"

"What big fight?"

"The one about the article you did on him in *Art in America*."

"Oh, *that*. It was just a spat. I see him all the time. You wouldn't believe their new loft. It's perfect."

This person, thought Connie, does not have one deep feeling about anything. She felt like a crabbed, bitter woman in a brittle curl over her coffee.

"You should give Alice a call—she'd love to hear from you."

"Alice was the one who stopped calling me, in case you don't remember."

"Connie, Alice loves you. She really does."

"Horseshit, Franklin. She stabbed me in the back."

"God, you girls are unbelievable. Girls are unbelievable."

They moved on, but from that point, Constance sat uneasily in her chair, no longer feeling like a woman entering a potentially successful phase in her career, happy in love and socially secure. She was, for several unpleasant moments, the isolated, lonely, insecure person she had been just three years earlier, a social blunderer, a locker-room towel for the maladjusted, unable to sell an article or figure out what to wear. Pull yourself together, she thought; it wasn't so bad.

But it had been. She cringed as they walked to the cash register, convinced that everyone was watching them and rolling their eyes.

"I'm giving a party the day after tomorrow," said Franklin as they walked out. "It's Emily's birthday. You've got to come. And bring your amour."

"Roger and Alice will be there."

"Oh, come on!"

"All right, I'll probably come. Give me your address."

He found a scrap of paper — the folded edge of a torn envelope — and scrawled his address in purple pen while the March wind raised his hair in an elegant, multidirectional headdress. A boy walked by in black leather, his bleached hair shaved into one strip down the center of his skull, painstakingly waxed and sculpted into the shape of a dragon's back. She felt a pang of affection and reassurance, knowing that kids were still doing the same things they'd been doing for years, tinged with a touch of incredulousness that they hadn't yet been able to think up anything else.

"Here." Franklin looked at her as he pressed the paper into her hand. "And Connie, I want you to know" — his eyes got that vague yet sincere and noble look they took on when he was about to talk about art or something — "I've thought about you a lot in the last year or so. I've really wanted to see you."

"Yeah?"

"Yeah. Really." His eyes looked so intensely vague, yet so sincere and so noble, she had the sense that the brown orbs could detach from their centers and wander all over his eyeball, slowly, with a certain majesty, each movement expressing the depth of his sincerity.

"You could've called me."

"Yeah, I could have. But I was too ashamed." He dropped his eyes and actually did look sincere for a minute.

She cupped his face with her hand and kissed his cheek. "Don't worry about it," she said.

They squeezed each other's hands, communicated some sexual comradery and goodwill, and then walked away.

Well, she thought, it was good to see Franklin, but she certainly wasn't going to his party. It would be too depressing. It was strange to realize that the depressing part wouldn't be her memory of his dizzy seduction attempt—she was never romantically interested in him anyway—but the presence of her ex-friend Alice, the mere mention of whose name had plunged her into a slight rancor. She eyed with disaffection and contempt the neatly hatted and booted, dyed and moisturized strangers marching toward her.

Alice and Roger had been the first New Yorkers she had met in Manhattan. They had met accidentally, when Constance had sublet their loft with two other girls. She had been very impressed by them. They were so handsome—Roger, blond and tall, his potentially annoying symmetry broken by the stubborn cowlick on the back of his head, and Alice, tiny and sleekly dark, her short hair like the shiny, pleated wings of a beetle, her clothes fully color-coordinated and accessorized—very poised, and apparently secure. Alice had asked her a lot of questions about her plans, and seemed to be scrutinizing her answers for signs of acceptability, while Roger smiled and nodded affably. At first Constance resented it, but soon, to her embarrassment, she found that she was flattered by Alice's eventual approval. Alice had been especially kind when Constance was thrown out of her first apartment after two days of tenancy with a psychotic roommate, rushing to her assistance with advice and a huge garbage bag of Salvation Army–bound clothes. "Don't leave New York because of this," she said. "Everybody gets mangled a little during the first few months."

She huffed up the five flights of stairs to her apartment, dropped the keys, swore unattractively and opened the door to find that the heat was too high, the cats were running around with mysterious desperation, and Deana wasn't home. The cats moiled loudly around her legs as she wrestled with can and opener; they squabbled for position as she put the blobs of cold meat-and-cornmeal by-products before them. "Oh, come on," she said. "You guys aren't that hungry. Pigs."

She went into the living area, turned on the radio to her favorite noncommercial station and was assaulted by horribly optimistic fiddle music. She thought: This must be the folk music slot. She snapped her tongue, turned it off and paced around the room. Their downstairs neighbor was whistling in a pealing, urgent way that usually drove her crazy but now seemed homey and reassuring simply because of its familiarity. She began to mentally list all the mean things that Alice had ever said or done to her. For example, the time Constance was overcome by a severe toothache, which turned out to be an exposed nerve, and had to walk out of a movie that she was watching with Alice. Alice had insisted on leaving with her, then complained all the way home about missing the movie. "Well, it was great riding the subway with you," she snapped as Constance staggered toward her building clutching her jaw.

But Alice wasn't just a straight-out bitch. It wasn't that simple.

Her neighbor rattled his castanets with ominous urgency. Constance slumped on the miserable old mattress that she and Deana had covered with fabric and large pillows and used as a couch. The mattress depressed her because it was like something that hippies would have in their apartment and because it was the same silly mattress that, in another life, had squeaked and rattled under the various activities of the two thousand and one dates. Yet, somehow she'd become attached to it, even though it was so mushy that when she sat on it it felt as if her internal organs were collapsing into one another. She collapsed across it now, supporting herself on one elbow planted deeply in the mattress, and surveyed the dustballs collecting under the desk and chair. No matter how often she and Deana swept, these animate-looking things slunk from corner to corner and left their residue on the cats' whiskers. The late afternoon light filtered in, eerie and faded through the gauzy float of dust, and cast an odd perspective on the room, at least from where she lay, making it look elongated and stark. The splintery floor looked craggy and forsaken with its dead dustball vegetation.

The cats, suddenly alert, ran to the door. There were footsteps, a key in the lock: Deana entered, encumbered by the cats.

"Boy, the guy downstairs is going bananas today," she said. She tossed her hair off her forehead with the usual nervous gesture. "Didn't you feed these guys?"

"Yeah, they just got their faces out of the dish two minutes ago." Connie rolled up and out of the mattress as gracefully as possible and put her arms around Deana's waist and her head on her shoulder.

"What's this?" Deana tenderly felt the lumps of Connie's spine, lingering in the spaces between the bones.

"Nothing. I was just spacing out and the room was beginning to look like a set for *Giant Ants from Pluto* or something."

"What?"

"I was in a weird mood."

"I guess so." Deana rubbed her briskly, let go and turned toward the refrigerator. "I'm starving. I have to have some carrots or something."

"What do you want for dinner?" Connie put one foot on the other knee and stood like an aborigine in a textbook photograph.

"I was thinking that we could order Chinese food from Empire. I'm too cranky to cook. And you're too weird to cook, apparently." She got the bag of carrots out of the refrigerator's vegetable bin and began scattering the sink with bright orange peels.

"Why are you cranky?"

"The same garbage. If I'd known I was going to work for a clone of my mother, I never would've taken the job." Deana rinsed her three shaved carrots meticulously, then went into the bathroom to tear off a large piece of toilet paper, folded it on the counter and put the carrots on it to drain. (One of her idiosyncrasies, which still caused Connie a pang of tender amusement, was her aversion to eating wet vegetables or fruit; she routinely dried pieces of cut fruit before putting them in her cereal.) "So what's your problem?"

Connie shrugged and sank into the mattress again. "I ran into somebody . . . not somebody I dislike really, just somebody I associate with anxiety."

"Who?"

"Somebody I haven't seen in years. Do you remember me mentioning Franklin Weston?"

Deana snapped off the end of a carrot. "Was he the guy you used to proofread with, who became some sort of quasi-famous art critic or something?"

"Yeah." Rat Fink, the male cat, came into grabbing range, and Constance scooped him into her lap like a large plush bunny, his eyes agog, paws helpless and limp in the air. "He's connected with some people I used to know before I met you. One person who—who hurt me, who rejected me in fact. Did I ever tell you about Alice?"

"A bit," said Deana, quietly crunching.

"Well, she came up in conversation and it depressed me. That's all." Rat Fink squeaked and flailed in her arms, wildly swatted his helpless tail, then jumped from her lap and hit the female cat on the nose. "The last time Alice and I talked was three years ago. It was when I was doing horribly, everything was going wrong, my writing was a disaster, I couldn't breathe, and I got so depressed that I couldn't eat. I was afraid to say anything about it to anyone and finally I decided to trust Alice enough to talk to her. Franklin kept saying 'Connie, Alice *loves* you,' in that stupid way he has, and I thought, Well, we've been friends for two years, so I told her. And she said, 'Connie, nobody wants to be around somebody who's unhappy.' She told me I should see a therapist, and never called me again. She didn't return my calls either."

"Why didn't you call her and yell at her?"

"I don't know. I didn't have the spirit, I guess. I felt pretty ravaged."

"It sounds like she was afraid of being unhappy herself," said Deana.

"Except that she didn't have anything to be unhappy about. She had—still has—a rich husband, a beautiful apartment, a pre-fabricated social life—"

"Oh, come on. Everybody has their sadness. And most people are scared of it. She sounds like one of those."

"All those clothes, those trips to Europe—sheer terror, I'm sure."

"Well, in any case, it doesn't sound like she was much of a friend. I'd say you were well rid of her."

"Yeah, I guess." Connie pulled herself out of the mattress, readjusted her weight and sank in at another angle. "It's just . . . the whole conversation was a vivid reminder of what it was like for me back then. Because of the thing with Franklin too. I don't remember if I ever told you about him, but just before the thing with Alice happened, he made this monstrous come-on to me, saying how much he loved me, going on and on about how beautiful and special I was, literally trying to drag me onto his mattress—it was bewildering, and I didn't quite trust it, and as it turned out, I was right. After a week of this he suddenly disappeared, and the next time I spoke to him, like two weeks later, he told me he was getting married to somebody named Emily, which he did."

"Another fine human being."

"But the thing about Franklin was that he had been a friend of mine up to that point. He virtually got me published in *New York* magazine. That's why it felt so awful. It was as if he and Alice had simultaneously decided—"

Deana left her carrots and, putting her fingers on Connie's lips, pitched the two of them into the center of the mattress. "God, you must be really depressed. I haven't heard you talk like this for ages." She stroked Connie's hair and smoothed her eyebrows. The mattress rasped and squeaked as they curled against each other like kittens in a shoe box.

"Franklin invited me to a party where Alice will be. I don't know what to do."

"Are you still thinking about that?"

They had just finished their take-out Chinese meal. Small white containers ranged over the table with fork handles protruding erectly from their centers; little balls of hardening rice trailed from container to plate; the cats circled beneath them with stiff, ardent steps. Deana was still lazily eating her spareribs and drinking her Vita-C.

"Connie, if this woman is such a bad memory, why don't you just forget it? Why dwell on her? She isn't in your life anymore."

Connie looked at the bright, cold flower of broccoli splayed prettily on the edge of her plate. "The thing is, Alice and I had a good time together. We'd go out to the movies, and then go for coffee and talk about the movie for hours, analyzing every character and gesture and the use of music and so on. I can remember when she ordered an anchovy sandwich and one of those sweet almond drinks and said, 'Whenever I'm with you I feel like eating stuff that's really fun and really bad for me.'"

"Hmpf," said Deana.

"And then there was the time that she and Roger paid for my airfare so I could visit them at their summer cottage in Pennsylvania."

"So why don't you go to Weston's party and see her?"

"Because there were other times when I felt she wasn't my friend at all. I remember her telling me about some big party she had that she didn't invite me to. She was complaining because she had wanted to have an equal number of highly successful males and females and she couldn't find enough successful females. It suddenly occurred to her that it was sort of rude to be talking about this in front of me when she hadn't even asked me to come, so she said, 'I didn't think of you because you're not in the field and you would've been bored anyway. I know you can hold your own on your own terms, but you couldn't deal with these people on their level.' Can you imagine?"

"Connie, were you in love with this woman?"

"What?"

"Did you have a thing for Alice?"

"No. Not at all. Why do you ask?"

"Because of the way you talk about it."

Connie paused and admired the graceful interaction of three long cold sesame noodles lying on her plate. "Well, it wasn't love, at least not romantic love. I'm just particularly sensitive to being betrayed by women. It's always been easy for me to be vulnerable around men because you're allowed to be. And I can make myself vulnerable to women sexually, but it's really hard to do with a woman friend. I did it with Alice and she rejected me."

Deana meditatively sucked a sparerib bone and limpidly blinked her large eyes.

Connie curled one leg up on the chair and sat on her ankle. "Once we went to see a movie about a dumb, trusting girl who gets involved with a whiny, sleazy psycho guy who tortures and kills her in the end."

"Great movie."

"Well, we wanted to see it because the actress had silicone implants and we wanted to see what they looked like. Anyway, Alice was so upset by this movie. She kept saying, 'That girl was so stupid, she deserved to die. You couldn't have any sympathy for her, she was so weak.'"

"That's not such an unusual reaction, you know." Deana plucked another slender red rib from its white box and began to delicately strip it of meat with her teeth.

"Okay, maybe not, but she got so obsessed about it, it was as if she was terrified at the mere idea that somebody could be a victim."

"Well, it is frightening."

Deana's voice was assuming the annoyed, panicky tone it got when she was having something ugly thrust upon her.

Connie turned and looked out the narrow window that opened onto an air shaft, a blackened brick wall and a wretched little window smothered in filthy cardboard and the scabrous rag of a dead curtain. The usual fat, dirty pigeons with bleary, beady eyes gathered on the opposite window ledge like unregenerate pimps. When they had first moved here, Constance worked very hard at seeing this view as something other than horribly depressing. "Just look at it," she'd tell herself. "Don't make a judgment."

"You have a way, you know, of shoving your vulnerability right into people's faces. Or something that you call vulnerability, anyway. You sometimes do it immediately upon meeting them. You force people to deal with it." Deana was speaking excitedly but precisely, her words like clean-cut vanilla-colored chips.

"Deana."

"No, listen to me. Don't be angry with me for saying this; you don't do it as much as you did. But you used to do it a lot, and it's kind of strange to be confronted so aggressively with somebody else's frailty. Some people will want to protect you, as I did, but some people will want to hurt you. Others will be merely afraid of you, for the obvious reason that it reminds them of their own frailty, which sounds a lot like your friend Alice."

Connie drew up her legs and sat with her arms around both knees and looked out the window again. It was true that in the summer the air shaft had an oddly poetic aspect. On days when the apartment air was heavy and stifling as a swamp, noises and smells came floating up it on clouds of heat, lyrical blends of voice and radio scraps, drifting arguments and amorous sighs, the fried shadow of someone's dinner, a faded microcosm that lilted into their apartment and related them to everyone else in the building. Of course, whether or not this relationship was a pleasant sensation depended largely on one's frame of mind, as well as on other factors; last summer the apartment below them had been sublet to a boy who would drunkenly imitate their voices when they made love.

"Have I upset you?" asked Deana.

"No, no." Connie looked up. "I understand what you're saying, but that wasn't the case with Alice. I never acted vulnerable around her. And actually I don't really agree with you. I may have done that to you because I responded to you sexually, but in general, I don't."

Deana shrugged. "Well, I only know what I've seen. I'm just trying to come up with an answer for you because you seem so distressed." She stood and collected the dishes. Her fingers and hands, Constance thought, had an exposed, strangely cold and receptive quality, like the nose of a puppy. As she was watching her clear the table and take the dishes to the kitchen, she could see the many aspects of her lover come forward and shyly recede with each movement; her rigid, stubborn arms, her strong shoulders positioned in a soft, demure curve, her stern chin, her luminous forehead, her odd way of stiffly holding back and gently, curiously moving forward—all spoke of her radial gradations of tenderness, sorrow and radiant, fanlike intelligence.

She woke up in the middle of the night, slumberously thinking of Franklin. *"I love you," he said. "I love you in a way I've never loved*

anyone." "I don't know what you mean," she said. "He's just crazed,"
said his friends. "Frank's hyper, that's all." What would happen if she
went to his party? Would he fall all over her and rave about how glad
he was to see her, then disappear for the rest of the night? Would it
hurt her feelings? She imagined Alice standing near a table of ravaged
snacks, holding a plastic cup of alcohol, a little hat neatly sitting on
her blow-dried head. It wasn't true that Alice had no unhappiness.
She had a schizophrenic mother who lived in a state mental hospital
(Alice's family wasn't wealthy) and who sometimes didn't know
her. Alice felt that she wasn't accepted as an artist by her circle, and
sometimes would get so upset about it that she'd scream and throw
things. "I feel like a piece of shit," she once said to Connie.

Connie turned and put her stomach and breasts against Deana's
warm back. She thought about the first woman she'd had a crush
on, a beautiful stripper with black hair and bitter blue eyes. She had
gone to see her strip and was irretrievably moved by the resigned but
arrogant turn of her strong chin, the way she casually offered and
rigidly withheld her body, as well as her tacky black lingerie.

"You don't love women. You're just trying to live out some
kind of porno fantasy invented by men with the corniest props
you can find," a gay woman had told her.

She turned again and placed her back in a matching curve against
Deana's. When she was a child, her mother had said, "When boys
get angry with each other, they just fight it out and it's all over.
But girls are dirty. They pretend to be your friend and go behind
your back." She remembered herself as the new girl in elementary
school trying to belong with the bony-legged clusters of little girls
snapping their gum and talking about things that she never discovered the significance of. She saw herself sitting alone in a high
school cafeteria eating french fries and a Cap'n Crunch bar.

She opened her eyes and could barely see the big-eared outline
of the tiny ceramic Siamese cat that her aunt had given her when
she was twelve. At the time she had thought that it and its brood
of ceramic kittens were the height of taste and elegance, and even
though its face had been broken in half and Krazy-glued back together, it still seemed faintly regal and glamorous. It had been one

of the items that Alice had in mind when she looked at Connie's dresser and said, "One of these days you're going to wake up and look at all this stuff and say, 'This doesn't have anything to do with me,' and throw it out."

But it does have something to do with me, thought Connie.

The next day she had to leave the office because of a sudden and painful toothache. She thought it might've been psychosomatically induced by the memory of the exposed-nerve episode with Alice in the theater, but the dentist assured her that it was not.

"Nope, nope, nope. This is the real thing, all right. You've just got a lulu of a mouth, is all. Just one thing after another. But this isn't a root canal. Just a deep, nasty filling." He jabbed her tooth with an instrument and she gasped with pain. "I'm surprised that it hasn't hurt you before. It's practically into your navel." He jabbed her again; she groaned and tried to close her mouth. "Don't worry, though, we caught it in time." He swiveled robustly in his chair and began to manipulate his precise, needle-nosed implements. Dr. Fangelli had very large forearms heavily strewn with hair; his hands seemed weirdly placed on his wrists, and his unevenly spaced fingers suggested undue activity in impossibly varied directions. He wasn't a big man, but when he walked his arms and shoulders rolled like a tank tread, and he seemed to suddenly require a lot of space.

"Okay, now, we're going to inject you with a little—" His face zoomed at her, and she had the disturbing thought that its happy, porous proximity could unhinge her jaw with the projected, exuberant desire that she open wide.

"What about the nitrous?" she asked.

He backed off. "Oh, I forgot, you like that. I keep telling you it kills your brain cells, but if you want it—" He swiveled violently away. "Carla! Carla, get me some nitrous in here, will you?"

Carla, a dark, small-nosed girl with mascara-crusted eyelashes, entered pushing the familiar gray machine, and a cool rubber, none-too-clean mask was placed over Connie's nose. "There we go," said Dr. Fangelli. "Crank her up, Carla. We'll let you get nice and relaxed. Carla, get the cream two-six base."

Connie closed her eyes. A balloon of warm air slowly expanded in her head. She thought of the commercials for Wonder Bread that she'd seen as a kid, in which a lucky little boy was borne by friendly butterflies to Wonder Bread Land, a place full of flowers and clouds and loaves of bread.

"So, Connie, are you married yet?" asked Dr. Fangelli.

"No."

"No? I'm surprised. How old are you?"

She lay in the chair like a starfish and imagined the sound of his voice, the clink of the instruments and the squeak of chairs penetrating her body with thin rays of light, piercing through her bones and traveling gaily up and down her skeleton. She imagined the very life force of the universe, in all its horrific complexity, penetrating her every pore, charging her body with millions of tiny beams. She sighed and inhaled deeply; she loved nitrous oxide.

"Okay, we've really got you flying now. Feel pretty good, doncha, Connie?"

Connie tried to surmount the saliva in her mouth and managed to make an affirmative noise. She could tell from the little oil slick on Dr. Fangelli's voice that he enjoyed seeing his patients helpless and openmouthed in his chair, that it made him feel powerful, and in fact, at this moment he *was* sort of powerful. Well, that was all right. The universe needed spaces for power to move into. It liked those spaces and valued them.

"Just a little pinch . . . there we go." He grabbed her lip and wriggled it. "You feel great, don't you? I bet we could take all your teeth out today and that would be fine with you. But of course, we're not going to do that." He patted Connie's shoulder. "It's just a small job that won't take a minute."

The problem was, if you're lying there like a starfish letting the universe seep through your pores, all kinds of stuff can get in. How do you keep out the bad things? *"Don't be such a Christian,"* *said Franklin. "Things aren't good or bad; they just are."* Well, that was a whole other line of thought. She pictured it as a wriggly, purple organism entering her space, and brusquely pushed it away. She tried to imagine a selective gray force field coming down at the various points on her body where the bad things were trying to enter. She became confused. Franklin wasn't altogether wrong. Buddhists and other people agreed with him. Anyway, even if you didn't agree with him, how could you tell for sure which things were bad? The tiny rubber hose sucking the spit from her mouth felt bad to her, as did the sound of the drill. But they weren't inherently bad, they were just dry and shrill. How did dryness and shrillness translate in terms of the universe? Surely these elements were affecting her nitrous oxide experience, but how?

Dr. Fangelli put some good, solid pressure on her tooth. "Carla, could you pass me the other drill?"

Then there were the basic things. She thought of Deana's soft, slightly fleshy embrace, the pale skin, the severe mouth, the tilt-eyed, heavy-framed glasses that made the composed, dignified face almost ludicrous. This was also one of the basic things: to lie in the dark under a blanket in an embrace with a tender lover, to have the sensations and their emotional entourage that came under the heading "sex." This was something that she contemplated with a feeling almost like relief, similar to how an exhausted person would view a vast, infinitely trustworthy pillow. You know what this is, everybody does. Like everybody knows what "job" and "success" mean. People who struggle for success are doing a primal thing. She had read something once about lab rats fighting for dominance, even under conditions where cooperation was needed for survival. She thought of herself at her desk reviewing manuscripts. She saw herself on the phone, talking to the editor of a piece that she'd recently completed. She felt detached as she viewed these images, which seemed more abstract than snapshots in a slide projector. They were like reminders scrawled on the square white days of a calendar. Like the imperative "call Fangelli for appt.," they were merely the most visible emblems, the crudest symbols for something too complex to describe in the given space. The image of herself at her desk, typing, became a scrawled notation for "job," but job was only another notation for something she barely sensed as a dark area of elements crossing and recrossing one another in an unreadable grid.

She made an effort to get out of the "work" area and saw herself lunching with her friend Helen, in the area marked "social life." Helen was talking about her boyfriend Patrick, who had strangled her a little bit the night before. "What I don't want to hear is how I don't deserve this," said Helen. "Last year when George hit me I remember telling some girl who kept saying, 'Helen, you deserve better than this,' which is just such a stupid thing to say, I mean, what does it mean?" Connie tried to remember if she had been the person to say this to Helen; it sounded like something she might say. Maybe it was a stupid thing to say, but it seemed as though *something* should be said. Helen still had faint blue bruises in her neck. "I said to him afterwards, like, were you trying to hurt me or something just now?"

This image—Helen frozen in her gestures with utensils and cigarette—receded into another dark corner of her fluid mental field, so that other scenes could crowd the picture. There was Connie, sometimes with Deana, sometimes alone, at a nightclub where a man was saying to her, "With that hat on, you look like you've got a piece of the world in your pocketbook," or at bars and parties, surrounded by well-dressed strangers who wielded their personalities like weapons and shields when they approached her, drinks in hand.

In confusion, she withdrew from all these things, which were, after all, only the substance of her life, and viewed them from a distance. Job, social life, relationship. Could these really be the things she did every day? What place was she in now, what was this distance from which they all looked so appalling? It felt like a blank space, silent and empty, so lonely that if she hadn't remembered it was all nitrous oxide–induced, she might've cried.

She opened her eyes and looked at the stiff black hairs on Dr. Fangelli's chin, and then at his placid, daydreaming gray eyes. Past them was the shiny, drab-colored machinery that was so forbidding to her but probably so familiar and homey to him. She shifted her gaze and met Carla's kind, squirrel-bright brown eyes. Was Carla's job in this office a set of symbols for her too, or was it an entity complete in itself, an efficient series of movements and interactions that emerged wholly and naturally from her needs and abilities like a bouquet of trick flowers, opening when you least expect it?

"Doing all right, aren't you?" asked Carla.

Connie made a faint affirmative half moan.

Carla made a small sensual laugh in her throat. "She's really enjoying herself now," she said.

"And we're allllmost done," said Dr. Fangelli. "Just a little . . ." He did some dull, painful thing that caused a nasty taste in her mouth.

She returned to her office in a mildly muddled state that was both combative and uncertain. She stopped in the ladies' room to look at herself in the mirror and saw with an unhappy loss of confidence that one side of her face had fallen into a jowly state of despair and that her eyes looked terribly tired and sad. She put on more makeup and entered the office. Luckily, there were only three people there, two assistants and an associate whom she liked.

On her desk was a copy of a story being considered for publication. She read it twice and took it into the associate editor's office.

"Steve," she said, "do you like this?"

"What's wrong with your mouth?"

"Ignore it. I look spastic, but I'm not, I just went to the dentist. Do you like this?"

"Yeah, I do. It's—"

"No, I mean really. Tell me the truth. Do you like this?"

Steve looked provoked, then cornered, then he marshaled himself. "Yes, Connie, I like it. It's terse, it's quirky, it tricks you into thinking you're safe, and then you find yourself on the edge of a cliff."

"Yeah, so does everything else we publish here."

"Connie, what do you want me to say? I know you feel frustrated about what we're publishing, but this is what Fulford likes. I don't have a problem with it."

"But I thought you liked the thing I showed you a few weeks ago."

"I did like it! I liked it a lot! But Fulford didn't."

"He never likes anything I like. I don't know why he hired me."

"You don't like many things. If you did blurbs for novels they'd read 'Mediocre! raves Constance Weymouth.'"

"You like everything."

"I'm ready to like things. That's true." He leaned back in his chair and tipped his head backward as if he were on a talk show hosted by an obnoxious crank. Then he banged his chair forward again and smiled.

They talked a little more; Steve said the quality of a text depended largely on the frame of reference you imposed on it. Connie disagreed. They made a few jokes and Connie went back to her cubicle. She sat quietly as her jaw woke up, and watched the coarsely sweatered back of an assistant move from side to side at her desk. Another assistant, a young, pretty woman who believed in what she was doing, distracted her by walking from one spot in the office to another, and Connie reflected that in a better state of mind she would be comforted by the slow, predictable sight of people engaged in meaningful activity. Now it induced ragged reverberations of her nitrous oxide experience, and she had an exhausting flashback of her haggard self carrying large chunks of her life, compressed into brightly colored packages that were marked "Constance the writer," "Constance the social being," "Constance as part of a couple"—all layering plain Constance alone in her apartment, waiting for Deana in the dark, under a blanket, arms wrapped around herself. She saw each marked package as a weight she carried back and forth, setting one down in a random spot so she could pick up another and stagger off in a new direction.

She put her head down on her desk.

On her way home from work she decided that she would go to Franklin's party.

"Why?" asked Deana. "After all this talk?"

"Because I feel like I need to end a cycle or something. Maybe I can get drunk and sock Alice."

"You're not serious, I hope."

"No. But I might stare her down."

"Well, I'm afraid I can't go with you if it's tomorrow. I have to have dinner with my mother at nine and after that I won't be fit for human society."

• • •

The party had apparently reached its peak an hour or two before she came. People looked as though they were bunched according to who grabbed whose arm on their way to the bathroom, and were leaning against walls, the women nodding their heads a lot. Some of them turned toward her and smiled with vague goodwill as she walked to the center of the room. She thought she recognized the lone couple dancing in a corner, eyes lowered in benign concentration as they shifted their weight from hip to hip and jogged their hands around their waists. She did recognize the man with hysterically bright blue eyes who was aggressively pacing around with a handful of greasy peanuts, and looked the other way.

"Connie, yo!" Franklin appeared with his hair in his eyes and his pores flowering magnanimously. "You came!" They groped for each other's hands and darted at each other's cheeks with a lot of "mm!" sounds.

"Where's your girlfriend?"

"Oh, she had a family obligation." They stood close, Connie quickly scanning the back of the room while Franklin's eyes wandered over her head. "Yo, Dave, I've gotta talk to you before you leave! Connie, the hooch is over there, there's some cake and stuff in the kitchen. And don't disappear! There's somebody I want to introduce you to." He squeezed her shoulder and moved away, and she penetrated more deeply into the crowd, heading for the discordant light-reflective arrangement of bottles and tumbling towers of paper cups. As she approached the table and reached for the slim neck of a vodka bottle, a woman turned around and she stood facing Alice. The neat proportions of surprise, warmth and compassion in the resulting declaration—"Connie!"—suggested that Alice had been prepared for this. She made a tentative half move with her upper body that looked like the first stage of a hug; Connie half moved in response and then stopped, so Alice stopped and they paused to look at each other, slowly recovering their distance. Connie wondered if Alice was inspecting her crow's-feet. "So, how've you been?" she asked. "How's your painting?"

"Good! I mean, I'm much more productive than I was when I

knew you. I don't spend half as much time tearing my hair out."

"Do you still have the feelings of resentment you had about Roger's success?" Alice's eyes slid sideways toward her with a short burst of expression that was like the gliding movement of a bird; this was a reference to their old discussions about Roger's commercial success and Alice's bitter jealousy.

"Yes, I do, but I've dealt with it. I'm not such a bitch about it. My own productivity has made it easier." They stood linked by a delicate membrane of remembered intimacy. "I hear your writing is going well."

"Yeah, it is." Connie listed the year's accomplishments, becoming for an annoying moment the girl from out of town who was trying to impress imperious Alice. The conversation was not what she had planned; they were talking like acquaintances at a party, perhaps because they were. "The magazine was fun at first," she finished. "But I'm not so happy there now. I don't have the influence that I thought I would. And it pays nothing."

"Still, it's a good spot, right? To make connections?"

"Yeah."

They stood looking in slightly different directions as the connective tissue began to dissolve in an anomaly of music and party chatter. Connie glanced sideways at Alice's face; there were tiny lines and a faint dryness that made her skin look frail, but the bone structure and demeanor still had the imposing, impenetrable look of a fashion model staring down a lifetime of cameras.

"How's your mother?" asked Connie.

Again there was the gliding appearance of open expression. "She died a few years ago. Just a little while after I talked to you last." Another threadlike connection stretched between them, but Connie wasn't sure what it was.

"That must've really been hard. I'm sorry."

Alice turned toward her, and Connie saw another face start to surface under the composed party expression, the careful eye makeup and poise. She wasn't sure how to define it, but it looked like the face of a young girl who had spent a lot of time studying models in fashion magazines.

"Yes, it was hard. You remember how things were. In a way I was relieved. But it was awful."

Somebody turned up the music and it marched between them.

"How're things with your parents?"

"Better." Connie nodded. "They're back together and the separation seems to have cleared the air. They actually seem to love each other again."

"Yeah? That's great." Alice turned toward the table, grabbed a large potato chip and used it to shovel up a mouthful of green paste. Connie found a paper cup without anything sticky on the inside and poured vodka into it. She groped for a bright sticky carton of orange juice and a brief storm of conversation bore them apart; Connie became embroiled with a very young man who wanted to talk about the magazine she worked for, while Alice was impaled by the aquamarine stare of the peanut-eater Connie had avoided. They were relieved to come together again a few minutes later in an opposite corner of the room.

"So Franklin tells me that you're living with a woman now."

"Yeah."

Alice's eyes brightened with a flare of enlightenment; she had never been able to understand Connie's manic affairs or the way she had flatly turned down the men Alice would introduce her to, and now here was the simple explanation: Connie was gay. "Is that good?"

"Yes, it is. I really love her."

"I'm glad to hear that."

"How're things between you and Roger?"

Alice looked away and shrugged. "Okay, I guess. We're not that close these days. He's seeing somebody else, actually. He's off somewhere with her tonight, I think."

"Oh!"

"It's not a crisis. I think that it's probably good for both of us. I'd be interested in an affair myself, but there's nobody around at the moment. Roger has a lot of access to single girls. He's gotten to be a pretty big deal, you know."

There was another shift in the surface of Alice's face and Connie saw a sudden resemblance to the person she'd seen in the mirror yesterday, right after her dental appointment—one half of the face was alertly contemplating the world with expectation and confidence, while the other had fallen under the weight of it. The eyes expressed the fatigue and rancor of a small, hardworking person carrying her life around on her back like a set of symbols and circumstances that she could stand apart from and arrange.

"Do you think that you'll stay married?"

"Oh, yes. I mean, my marriage with Roger is like . . . a project I'd never drop. And I want to have children soon."

Connie looked at the sadness in her jaw and the tired eyes, and she wanted to put her arms around Alice, to hold her and comfort her. Then either the face or her perception changed, and she was once again looking at a handsome, self-assured, wealthy woman with polite, curious, impenetrable eyes. "You know that we moved, don't you? We bought a wonderful co-op in Soho. We'll be having a party sometime soon. I should invite you."

"Oh, Alice!" A man in a paisley jacket with a smile like a bludgeon swooped toward them and took Alice's elbow. "I must introduce you to Alex here. . . . Hi," he said to Connie. "Are you a painter too?"

Connie said no, and Alice waved a tiny good-bye with her fingers and went to meet Alex. Connie walked into the next room with her drink and got a hunk of chocolate cake and stood eating it out of one hand, dropping crumbs on the floor. A man asked her if she was a writer and she got involved in drunken conversations with three different people, in which almost nothing was said. The last was interrupted when Franklin appeared, his eyelids thick and purple, and took her by the arm. "Here's a woman you've just got to meet. She's incredibly intelligent and she's a writer for *The New Yorker.* Cathy! Cathy! This is Constance Weymouth, an incredible writer, one of the most brilliant writers I know. You've got a lot to talk about."

An attractive gray-haired woman with large blue eyes stood facing her uncertainly but gamely. Connie shook her hand and they traded magazine gossip until it became apparent that while a great friendship could possibly be forged between them, the present situation precluded it.

Two more couples shifted and undulated in the corner, and Connie watched them with a mournful and diffuse concentration. Their flat-footed steps were neither graceful nor dynamic, but their goodwill infused their clumsy gestures—the hand outstretched to squeeze a partner's hand, the sudden eye contact—with a gentle, faded romance that made Connie want to go home and be with Deana.

She found Franklin in the middle of two conversations about sculpture and Libya and said good-bye to him quickly. As she was putting on her coat, Alice turned toward her and smiled, holding a finger up in the paisley man's face. "Are you leaving?" She came hurriedly across the floor. "Do you want to wait a little while? I'm going soon."

Connie felt an eagerness light in her eyes and then fade. She hesitated.

"Well, if you're in a rush, go ahead. But here, let me give you my card." Alice had her business card ready in her hand. "It's our new phone number. Why don't you call?"

They said it was good seeing each other, made more stunted hugging gestures and settled for hand squeezes.

Connie walked three blocks before hailing a cab. "You think you know what you're doing, but you don't," a huddled drunk informed her. She gave him a dollar bill and walked on, silently agreeing. Why hadn't she waited for Alice? *"Alice loves you, Connie," Franklin had said.* A couple across the street were embracing against a crumbling brick wall; the man's hand was under the woman's short leather skirt. Because she'd been ending a cycle and they weren't friends anymore, Constance thought. She stopped before a garbage-choked wastebasket and pulled Alice's card from her pocket. She started to throw it away and then changed her mind. You never know. One day she might come upon this card and decide it would be good to talk to somebody she hadn't spoken to in years. She pocketed the little piece of cardboard and hailed a cab that was roaring down the street like a desperate animal.

Heaven

WHEN VIRGINIA THOUGHT of their life in Florida, it was veiled by a blue-and-green tropical haze. Ocean water lapped a white sand beach. Starfish lay on the shore and lobsters awkwardly strolled it. There was a white house with a blue roof. On the front porch were tin cans housing smelly clams and crayfish that walked in circles, brushing the sides of the cans with their antennae; they had been brought by her son Charles, and left for him and his brother, Daniel, to squat over and watch from time to time.

She imagined her young daughters in matching red shorts, their blond hair pulled back by rubber bands. The muscles of their long legs throbbed as they jumped rope or chased each other, rubber thongs patting their small, dirty heels with every step. A family picnic was being held in the front yard on an old patchwork quilt. Watermelon juice ran down their sleeves.

Jarold was holding Magdalen in the ocean so she could kick and splash without fear. He was laughing, he was pink; his hair lay in wet ridges against his large, handsome head.

Twenty years later, Virginia thought of Florida with pained and superstitious but reverent wonder, as though it was a paradise she had forfeited without knowing it. She thought of it almost every night as she lay on the couch before the humming, fuzzing TV set in the den of their New Jersey home. She lay with her head on a hard little throw pillow, staring out of the picture window into the darkened back yard at the faint glimmer of the rusting barbecue tray. She thought that if they had stayed in Florida, her son would still be alive. She knew it didn't make any sense, but that's what she thought.

When Virginia met Lily, her fifteen-year-old niece, Lily had said to her, "Grandmother used to tell us about you all the time. She said you could pick oranges in your back yard. She said you once found a lobster walking in your living room. She said there'd be tornadoes and your house would flood, and horrible snakes would come in. You sounded so exotic. It didn't seem like you could be related to us."

They were riding in the warm car with their seat belts on. Virginia had just picked Lily up at the Newark airport because Lily was coming to live with them.

Virginia had been charmed by her remark.

Lily's mother was visiting Jarold and Virginia. It had been almost eight years since Virginia had spent so much time with her sister.

Anne was the short, brown-haired sister to two tall blondes, a nervous, pitifully conscientious child who always seemed to be ironing or washing or going off somewhere with an armload of books. Her small mouth was a serious line. Her large gray eyes were blank and dewy. She often looked as though she was about to walk into a wall.

Since Anne was the oldest by five years, their mother made her responsible for the care of Virginia and Betty on weekends, when she went into Lexington to clean houses for rich people. Anne accepted the responsibility with zeal. She rose early to get them eggs and milk for breakfast, she laid the table with exquisite care, wreathing the plates with chains of clover. Virginia and Betty complained when she dragged them out of bed to eat; they made fun of her neat breakfast rituals. They refused to help her with the dishes.

Anne dated only scholarly boys. She spent earnest, desperate hours on the porch with them, talking about life and holding hands. She'd bound up the stairs afterward, her eyes hotly intent, her face soft and blushing with pleasure. Her sisters would tease her, sometimes until she cried.

At forty-eight, Anne had become plump, homely and assured. Her eyes had become shrouded with loose skin and she wore large beige glasses. Her eyebrows had gotten thick, but her pale skin was fine and youthful.

During the visit it was Anne who made charming, animated conversation with Jarold and Magdalen. It was she who laughed and made them laugh on the canoe trips and barbecues. Virginia sat darkly silent and meek, watching Anne with interest and some love. She knew Anne was being supportive. Anne had been told that Virginia had not recovered well from Charles's death, and had come to bring lightness to the darkened house. She was determined to cheer Virginia, just as she'd been determined to mop the floor or make them eat their breakfast.

She had approached Lily with the same unshakable desire to rectify.

Lily's presence in Virginia's life began as a series of late-night phone calls and wild letters from Anne. The letters were full of triple exclamation points, crazy dashes or dots instead of periods, violently underlined words and huge swirling capital letters with tails fanning across several lines. "Lily is so withdrawn and depressed." "Lily is making some very *strange* friends." "Lily is hostile." "I think she may be taking drugs . . ." "Think she needs help—George is resisting—may need recommendation of a counselor."

Virginia imagined the brat confronting her gentle sister. Another spoiled, pretty daughter who fancied herself a gypsy princess, barefooted, spangled with bright beads, breasts arrogantly unbound, cavalier in love. Like Magdalen.

"I want to marry Brian in a gypsy wedding," said Magdalen. "I want to have it on the ridge behind the house. Our friends will make a circle around us and chant. I'll be wearing a gown of raw silk with a light veil. And we'll have a feast."

"Does Brian want to marry you?" asked Virginia dryly.

Magdalen was seventeen. She had just returned home after a year's absence. She carried a fat green knapsack on her back. Her feet were filthy. "I'm coming home to clear my head out," she said.

She ate huge breakfasts with eggs and bacon, baked a lot of banana bread and lay around the den playing with tarot cards. Family life went on around her brooding, cross-legged frame. Her long blond hair hung in her face. She flitted around with annoying grace, her jeans swishing the floor, humming songs about ladies on islands.

After six months she "decided" to marry Brian, and went to Vancouver to tell him about it.

Virginia was glad to see her go. But, even when she was gone, insistent ghosts of Magdalen were everywhere: Magdalen at thirteen, sharp elbows on the breakfast table, slouching in an over-long cashmere sweater, her sulky lips ghoulish with thick white lipstick—"Mom, don't be stupid, everybody wears it"; twelve-year-old Magdalen, radiant and triumphant, clutching an English paper graded triple A; Magdalen in the principal's office, her bony white legs locked at the ankle, her head primly cocked—"You've got a bright little girl, Mrs. Heathrow. She should be moved at least one year ahead, possibly two"; Magdalen lazily pushing the cart at the A&P, wearing yellow terry-cloth shorts and rubber sandals, her chin tilted and her green cat eyes cool as she noticed the stock boys staring at her; fifteen-year-old Magdalen, caught on the couch, her long limbs knotted up with those of a long-haired college freshman; Magdalen, silent at the dinner table, picking at her food, her fragile nostrils palpitating disdainfully; Magdalen acting like an idiot on drugs, clutching her mother's legs and moaning, "Oh, David, David, please make love to me"; Magdalen in the psychiatrist's office, her slow white fingers dropping cigarette ashes on the floor; Jarold, his mouth like a piece of barbed wire, dragging a howling Magdalen up the stairs by her hair while Charles and Daniel watched, embarrassed and stricken.

For years Magdalen had overshadowed two splendid boys and her sister, Camille. Camille sat still for years, quietly watching the gaudy spectacle of her older sister. Then Magdalen ran away and Camille emerged, a gracefully narrow-shouldered, long-legged girl who wore her light-brown hair in a high, dancing ponytail. She was full of energy. She liked to wear tailored blouses and skirts, but in home economics she made herself a green-and-yellow snakeskin jumpsuit, and paraded around the house in it. She delighted her mother with her comments: "When boys tell me I'm a prude, I say, 'You're absolutely right. I cultivate it.'" She was not particularly pretty, but her alert, candid gaze and visible intelligence made her more attractive than most pretty girls. When Virginia began to pay attention to Camille, she could not understand how she had allowed Magdalen to absorb her so completely. Still, there were ghosts.

Magdalen had been gone for over a year when Anne called. It was a late summer night. Virginia and Jarold were in the den watching *Cool Hand Luke* on TV. The room was softly dark, except for the wavering white TV light. The picture window was open. The cool night air was clouded with rustlings and insect noises. Virginia sat with her pink sweater loose around her shoulders, against Jarold's arm. Their drinks glimmered before them on the coffee table. Virginia's cigarette glowed in a metal ashtray. Their sparerib dinner had been lovely.

Charles called her to the phone, and she felt a thrill of duty. What had happened to Lily now? She took her drink and cigarettes and left the gentle darkness, padding down the hall and through the swing door into the kitchen. The light was bright and there was a peaceful smell of old food. She shooed Charles, who was eating a dish of lime sherbet at the counter, and sat on the high red stool under the phone, her elbows on her knees. "What is it, honey?"

Lily had just been released from a mental hospital. "All she does is lie around like a lump, eating butter sandwiches and drinking tea like a fiend. I don't think she can go back to school here, now that she's been expelled. We've already tried sending her away to school and that didn't work either. I don't know what to do."

Magdalen was somewhere in Canada. Camille was away at college. Charles and Daniel were always outside playing. "Why doesn't Lily come and go to school here?" she said. "I'm fresh out of girls, you know. Send her on out."

She went back into the den forty minutes later. Jarold was hunched forward on the couch with the exasperated expression that he always had when he was watching liberals on TV. He was so intent on *Cool Hand Luke* that he didn't ask about the telephone call. She cuddled against him silently.

She meant to tell him about Lily after the movie was over, but she didn't. She planned to tell him for several days. Then she realized she was putting it off because she knew he would say no.

So she decided not to tell him anything. All week, she fantasized about Lily, and what it would be like to have her there.

A week later, she picked Lily up at the airport. As she stood shielding her eyes to scan the passengers climbing from the plane, she realized that she had been vaguely expecting Lily to look like Magdalen. She felt a slight shock when she noticed the small, pale, brown-haired girl. Even as Virginia adjusted her expectation, she was surprised by Lily's appearance. She had not imagined such a serious face. As Lily came toward her among the passengers, Virginia felt an odd sense of aloneness about the girl. Her gray eyes were wide and penetrating, but seemed veiled, as if she wanted to look out without you looking in. Her mouth and jaw were stiff and rather pained. Virginia was curious and taken aback.

She bought Lily a can of grape pop and took her to the car. It was a humid day; the seats were sticky and hot. They rolled down all the windows, and Virginia turned on the radio to a rock station. Lily didn't say much until they got out on the turnpike. Then she said the thing about Florida. Virginia was surprised and pleased. She laughed and said, "Well, we did chase a few lobsters around the house, but it would take more than that to make us exotic. We just couldn't manage to keep the doors and windows shut at the same time."

"Maybe exotic isn't the right word," said Lily. "You were just so obviously different from us. Mother showed us pictures of you and you always seemed so self-assured. I remember a picture of Magdalen and Camille. They were both standing with their hips out and one of them—Magdalen, I guess—had her foot perched up on something. They looked so blond and confident."

Virginia thought of the pictures she had seen of Anne's family. In a group, they looked huddled together and meek, even when they were all smiling brightly. They looked as though they were strangers to the world outside their family, as if they had come out blinking, wanting to show their love and happiness, holding it out like a shy present. Anne's daughters were pretty in a different way from Magdalen or Camille. She remembered a picture of Lily and her sister Dawn crouching in a sandbox in frilly red sunsuits. Their brown hair just reaching their shoulders, and the bashful smiles on their bright, thin lips seemed heartbreakingly, dangerously fragile to her.

"Well, you all looked darling to us," she said. "We could tell you were sweet as pie."

Virginia left the highway and took Lily for a drive through the mountains. She drove to the top of a hill that looked down on a lake and some old dull-colored green pines. They were near a convent, and the woods were planted with white daisies and small purple flowers. They got out and walked until Virginia felt a light sweat on her skin. Then they sat on a stone bench near the convent and told each other family stories. Virginia liked Lily. She was intrigued by her. She wondered why such an intelligent child could not do well in school.

They went home and Virginia made them cups of tea.

Charles and Daniel came home from school. They were surprised to see Lily, and to hear that she was coming to live with them. They sat at the table and Virginia served them pieces of coconut cream pie. The three children had a short, polite conversation. Charles said, "That's a cool knapsack. My sister Magdalen has one like that."

When the boys went upstairs, Virginia began to worry. Jarold was coming home, and she still hadn't thought of what to say to him.

She decided to take a shower and put on a pretty blouse. She told Lily to make herself at home, and went upstairs. When she came down again, she found Jarold in the kitchen; he had left work early. He was standing at the table, his face red and bitterly drawn about the eyes. He looked at Virginia like she was his enemy. Lily looked at her too, her face stiff and puzzled. Jarold walked out of the room.

She and Jarold talked about it that night. Apart from the intrusion, Jarold did not like Lily. "She's weird," he said. "She has no social graces. She just stares at you." They were lying in bed on their backs in their summer pajamas, their arms lying away from their bodies in the heat. The electric fan was loud.

"Jarold, she's shy," said Virginia. "And she's upset. She's had a hard time these last few months."

"Whose fault is that? Why do we have to get stuck with her hard time, Virginia? Answer me that."

Virginia lay still and looked at her long naked feet standing at the end of the bed. She couldn't think of an answer.

"And she's got such a pasty little face," continued Jarold. "She looks like something that crawled out from under a rock."

"Jerry." Her voice was soft and blurry in the fan.

"I don't think Jarold likes me," said Lily the next day.

Virginia was doing the dishes. Lily stood beside her, leaning against the wall, standing on one leg.

"He just needs time to get used to you." Virginia dug around in the water for the silverware and tried to think of something to say. "He told me last night that you remind him of Magdalen. And he loved Magdalen."

Virginia could feel Lily brightening.

"But you see, Magdalen hurt him more than anyone else in the world. It's a painful memory for him."

"I guess so," said Lily. "He told me I look like something that crawled out from under a rock."

Jarold was a big, handsome man who sold insurance to companies. His handsomeness was masculine and severe. His bright blue eyes were harsh and direct, and his thin, arched eyebrows gave him an airy demon look that was out of character with his blunt, heavy voice. He rarely made excessive or clumsy movements, although his walk was a little plodding. He had become successful very quickly. They had never been forced to live in small apartments with peeling wallpaper. For years Virginia believed that Jarold could surmount anything. He could, too, until Magdalen.

Jarold had been in love with Magdalen. At breakfast, he would look at her as she sullenly pushed her egg around her plate while the other children chattered, as if her bored, pale face gave him the energy to go to work. He read all of her papers from school; he always wanted to take her picture. She could make him do anything for her. He'd let her stay out all night; he let her spend the weekend in New York when she was fifteen. Wherever she was, even when she was traveling around Canada with a busload of hippies and a black person, if she cabled home for money, Jarold sent it immediately. If he tried to be strict, she would tease and flatter him. The few times he lost his temper and punished her, she punished him with silence. When he dragged her up the stairs and spanked her, she ran away from home. She called a week later and spoke to Virginia, but she hung up when Jarold got on the phone. It was the first time that Virginia had seen Jarold cry.

"Magdalen has real charm," said Jarold to Lily. "She can charm the birds off the trees. You don't have any of that. You don't have any personality at all."

Virginia was surprised at the intensity of Jarold's dislike for Lily. And, although Lily never expressed it openly, Virginia felt that Lily hated him too. Lily never argued with him; she barely acknowledged his presence. When she had to speak to him, her voice was clipped and subtly condescending, as though he were beneath defiance.

One evening, Lily and Virginia were sitting together in lawn chairs in the back yard when Charles and Daniel approached them with a big piece of wood. The boys had shot four squirrels, skinned them and nailed the skins to it. They displayed the skins proudly, and Virginia praised them. Lily said nothing until they left. Then she said that she thought it was sick.

"I know, it seems awful," said Virginia. "But they're little boys and it means something to them. They do it to impress their father." Virginia was unnerved by the sudden look of contempt on Lily's face.

"I know," she said.

Lily's stay gradually became more and more unpleasant and eventually became a discomfiting memory that hung over the house for quite a while. But there were bright spots that stood out of the unpleasantness so vividly that they seemed to come from somewhere else altogether.

Virginia would spend afternoons with Lily after school. They'd change into jeans and T-shirts and drive into the mountains where they'd gone the first day. Sometimes they'd stop at a Dairy Queen and buy pink-spotted cups of ice cream in melting puddles of syrup. They'd sit on the car hood, slowly swinging their legs and eating the ice cream with pink plastic spoons, talking about the bossy girl in Lily's home ec class, or the boy she thought was "different." Virginia spoke about her high school days, when she was beautiful and popular and all the girls tried to be friends with her. She'd give Lily social advice about how to choose her friends.

When they'd get to the mountains, they'd leave the car and walk. They'd become quiet and concentrate on the walk. They'd find paths, then break branches from trees and use them to clear their way. Lily would stop to examine plants or insects, her brow taut and puzzled. She'd pick up a lot of things to hold in her pockets, especially chestnuts. She would pick up a chestnut and hold it in her hand for the whole walk, stroking it with her fingers, or meditatively rubbing it across her lower lip.

Other times they'd just sit at the kitchen table and drink tea. Virginia was astonished at the things she told Lily during these afternoons. Lily knew things about Virginia that very few other people knew. Virginia did not know why she confided in her. She had been lonely. The afternoon kitchen was sunny and lulling. Lily listened intently. She asked questions. She asked a lot of questions about Magdalen.

"But don't you like Magdalen?" she asked once. "Weren't there good times when she was growing up?"

"Magdalen could be the most lovely, charming child in the world—if she wanted to be. She'd give you the shirt off her back—if she was in the mood. *If* she was in the mood. But to answer your question, no, I don't like Magdalen. I love her—I love her dearly—because I'm her mother and I can't help it. But I don't like her."

Lily stared at her, pale and troubled.

"Don't you ever repeat that. It's very private. If Magdalen ever comes to me and says, 'Mama, Lily says you don't like me,' I'll say you're lying."

As they talked, Lily rested her elbow on a small pile of school-books. She carried these books to and from school every day. One of them had a split green cover that showed its gray cardboard stuffing and a dirty strip of masking tape running up its broken spine. Whenever Lily heard Jarold pull into the driveway, she would grab her books and leave the room. Jarold would come in and see her cup on the table, its faint sugary crust fresh around the bottom. He'd never say anything, but his mouth got sarcastic.

Virginia tried to get Jarold to be nicer to Lily. "She's got a special kind of charm," she said. "She's gentle and low-key. She listens, and she has fresh insights." Sometimes Jarold looked as though he were listening to this.

But Lily wouldn't or couldn't show Jarold her charm. To him, she displayed only her most annoying aspects. And they really were annoying. She almost never said anything at family meals; she either kept her head down and chewed, or stared at people. She ignored Jarold, and sometimes she ignored Virginia too. She was judgmental; she was always talking about what was wrong with the world. She never helped with the dishes or anything else. She was always going into the refrigerator and eating the last piece of pie or cheesecake or whatever dessert was there. She'd say weird things, and when you'd ask her to explain what she meant, she'd say, "Oh, never mind." She'd sit around looking as if somebody had been beating her with a stick. She'd droop on the wall. She was depressing.

In September, Lily would sit with her books on the floor of the den at night, reading and underlining sentences with fat turquoise lines. Virginia would be on the couch reading the paper, her square brown glasses on the end of her nose. The TV would be on, usu-ally a talk show neither of them wanted to see. On the coffee table there'd be a fat economy-size jar of olives, which they both ate from. They'd talk intermittently, and Virginia liked to think that her silent presence was an encouragement to Lily's studying.

In September, Lily got good grades on her quizzes. Her art teacher said nice things about her drawings. She got an A-plus on a humanities paper, and the teacher read it aloud to the class. Virginia called Anne and read it to her.

During October, Lily stopped studying on the floor of the den. She left her broken-backed books on the couch and went upstairs to her room and shut the door. Virginia could hear the radio playing behind the door for hours. She wondered irritably what Lily was doing in there.

On weekends her long-haired friends would come to the door and she'd disappear for the entire day. At night they'd hear the screen door slam, and Lily would pat through the den, her bell-bottoms swishing, her face distantly warm and airy. She'd float down the hall without a word.

The second week in October, Mr. Shin, the school disciplinarian, called Virginia. He told her that Lily was rude in the classroom and that she used obscene language. Two weeks later he called again, this time to say that he thought Lily was taking drugs.

Virginia thought Mr. Shin had a repulsive voice. She thought he was deliberately persecuting Lily for reasons having nothing to do with obscene language or drugs. Lily once said that Mr. Shin told her that her IQ was below normal, that she belonged in a mental hospital, and that he didn't blame her parents for not wanting her. At first Virginia was angry. She thought of telling Jarold to call Mr. Shin and tell him to leave Lily alone. But then she realized that Jarold was in agreement with him. Then she felt embarrassed. After all, Mr. Shin was right, Lily did use obscene language, casually and often. She did take drugs.

It was Lily's birthday. Jarold was out of town on business. Daniel and Charles had bought her a deck of tarot cards and a pair of earrings. There was a boxed cake in the refrigerator. Virginia was going to ask Lily what she wanted for dinner, but when Lily came home she was too high to answer the question. She tried to act normal, but she couldn't She said weird things and giggled. Lily almost never giggled; it was a strangely unpleasant sound.

Virginia sent the boys to visit their friends next door. Then she turned to Lily. "You are a constant irritant," she said. "I'll never forgive Anne for dumping you on me, although the poor woman was probably desperate to get rid of you." She didn't remember what she said after that. She was furious, so it probably wasn't very nice. She recalled that Lily said nothing, that she seemed to shrink and become concave. She kept pulling her hair in front of her mouth and holding it there.

It was very different from the way Magdalen had acted when Virginia would catch her on drugs. Virginia could scream at Magdalen, and call her anything she liked. Magdalen would follow her around, her long legs working in big strides, eyes blazing. she'd yell, "Mom! Mom, you know that's a bunch of shit. What about the time you . . ."

But Lily just sat there, becoming more and more expressionless.

Virginia slept with Lily that night. She went into her room, no longer angry but with a sense of duty, concerned that Lily know she was cared for, that she wouldn't go through the drug experience alone.

She found her lying on the bed with all her clothes on, staring. Virginia made her change into her nightgown and get under the blankets. She turned out the light and got into bed with her. Lily went into a tight curl and turned her face to the wall. Virginia got the impression that she didn't understand why Virginia was there.

Virginia said, "Well? Don't you want to talk?"

Lily didn't answer for a long time. Then she said, "About what?"

"Whatever's on your mind."

Another long pause.

"There's nothing on my mind."

Her words sounded disconnected, not only from her but from each other. Virginia suddenly wanted her to go home, back to Michigan. It would be easy. All she had to do was tell Jarold that she'd been taking drugs.

"Well, that's funny. Magdalen was a talker."

"About what? What did she talk about?" She sounded genuinely interested.

"Oh, about boys. There was one in particular. David. I remember the name because she kept moaning it over and over." She hadn't meant to sound sarcastic, but it was hard not to.

Lily didn't say anything.

They lay there in silence, not even scratching or shifting. Every time one of them swallowed, it was obvious that she was trying to do it quietly. Virginia's nightgown was hot and her feet were dry. She felt as if she couldn't close her eyes. She remembered the afternoon conversations they had shared and their walks in the mountains. They seemed meaningless now—like bits of color glimpsed through a kaleidoscope. She felt an unhappy chill.

Virginia turned, and the blankets rasped in the long silence. In a fiercely sudden move, she put her body against Lily's, and her arm around her. She waited, almost frightened.

For several seconds there was no reaction. Then Virginia could feel every muscle in Lily's body slowly tightening. Lily's body became rigid. Her back began to sweat.

They lay like that, uncomfortably, for a long time. Having moved, it was hard for Virginia to turn away again.

The next day they ate birthday cake from paper plates on their laps as they watched TV. Jarold said, "Well, do you feel fifteen?"

"I don't know," said Lily.

It seemed like she really didn't know. She looked badly shaken. Jarold didn't say anything else. Charles stopped eating his cake and looked at Lily for a long moment. He looked puzzled and disturbed; for one thing, Lily loved cake and she hadn't eaten any of the cake in her lap.

Virginia didn't tell Jarold about the drugs, but he got rid of Lily anyway. She had stayed out with her friends one night, and he had her things packed when she came back the next morning. They drove her to the airport within the hour and left her waiting for a standby flight with her clothes in a big white shopping bag. Virginia kissed her good-bye, but it didn't feel like anything.

That night Anne called. Lily had not gone home. She had taken a plane to Canada instead. "I don't think we'll send anybody after her this time," said Anne. "It wouldn't do any good. Nothing we ever did was any good."

"Don't blame yourself," said Virginia.

For a few days afterward, Jarold talked about how awful it had been to have Lily there. Then he forgot about it. Charles was the last person to mention her. It was shortly after Virginia got a call from Magdalen. He said, "You and Dad were always acting like Lily and Magdalen were alike. But they weren't anything alike at all.

For a while after that, life was okay. Magdalen was still acting like an idiot, but seemed to have stabilized in a harmless way; she had a steady job as a waitress in a health-food restaurant in South Carolina, and talked about astral travel and crystal healing when they called her. Camille was in law school at Harvard. She was engaged to a handsome, smiling med student. She sent glorious twelve-page letters to her mother on multicolored stationery covered with purple or turquoise ink. She described her teachers and her friends. She wrote about how much she loved Kevin, how much she wanted to have children and a career. She recorded her dreams and the art exhibits she'd seen. Virginia imagined Camille sitting at her desk in class. Her legs were folded restfully before her, her body slouched with arrogant feminine ease, but her neck was erect and her large eyes watchful. She imagined her sitting at an outdoor café, her bony knees childishly tilted together under the table, her long hands draped on top of her warm coffee cup as she leaned forward, laughing with her friends. She saw Camille walking across campus with Kevin. His brown jacket was loose on her shoulders, protecting her.

Daniel and Charles grew up easily. They trooped around the house with noisy bunches of boys who all seemed to have light, swinging arms and stinging, nasty voices. At times their eyes were dull and brutish. They told cruel, violent jokes and killed animals. They were mean to other children. But they harbored a sweetness and vulnerability that became exposed at unexpected moments. And they were still her little boys. She could hear it in the way Charles called, "Mom?" when he couldn't sleep at night. She would pass by his room and hear his voice float plaintively from the darkness. She would look in and see him sitting up in his gray-and-white pajamas, slim and spare against the headboard, his blond hair standing up in pretty spikes. She would sit on his bed for at least an hour. Sometimes she would lift up his pajama top and gently scratch his warm back. He loved that.

When Daniel was fifteen, he found a girlfriend. She was fourteen. she was very short and had dark hair and gentle hands. She had a round, sweet face and worried eyes. She worried about things like ecology. She sat in the kitchen with Daniel after school, eating Virginia's sandwiches and talking about the EPA and whales. Her feet, in striped tennis shoes, barely touched the floor. Daniel admired her as he ate his sandwich. He stopped killing squirrels with BB guns.

When Charles was twelve, he was in a school play. He was one of the Lost Boys in the high school production of *Peter Pan*, a boy named Tootles. It was a small part, and he was nonchalant about it, but he loved to dress in his contrived rags and make his eyes fiendish with black eye paint. He came home from rehearsal that way. Virginia would see a beam of light in the driveway, then hear a car door slam and muffled voices. The door would bang and Charles would appear, nimbly swaggering in his frayed knickers and flapping sleeves. He'd grab something to eat from the kitchen and wheel into the den, yelling his lines in a mocking voice. "You see, sir, I don't think my mother would like me to be a pirate. Would your mother like you to be a pirate, Slightly?"

She went to the play on opening night and sat in the front row with Jarold and Daniel. Charles was vibrant on stage. His airy movements had more authority than anyone else's in the cast, except the lead. She couldn't take her eyes off him. The pale little girl playing Wendy lay fainting before him in her white nightgown, her long brown hair fanned across his feet. He said, "When ladies used to come to me in dreams I said, 'Pretty mother, pretty mother.' But when at last she really came, I shot her." Tears came to her eyes. She looked at Jarold and saw him smiling and blinking rapidly. Charles said, "I know I am just Tootles and nobody minds me. But the first who does not behave to Wendy like an English gentleman, I will blood him severely."

When the play ended, Virginia went to the dressing room. It was an old classroom with heavy wooden mirrors propped against the walls and cardboard boxes full of makeup and cold cream on the desks. Children were leaping around the room, chattering and singing songs from the play in sarcastic voices. They were bright-eyed and demonic when seen up close. Virginia saw Charles. She saw him dip his hand into a jar of cold cream, turn and slap it across a timid-looking girl's face. The girl smiled painfully and tried to laugh. Another girl pointed at her and laughed. Charles turned away.

She dreamed of a conversation with Lily. They were sitting at the kitchen table with cups of tea before them. She said, "After I had Daniel, the doctors told me that I shouldn't have any more children. They said it would be unsafe. I was lying there in the hospital when they came in and announced, 'While we've got you here, we're going to tie your tubes.' And I said, 'Oh, no, you're not.' I wouldn't let them do it. and the next year I had Charles." She smiled foolishly at Lily.

The dream-Lily smiled back. "Charles is a beautiful boy," she said. "I think he may be a genius in a way people don't yet under-stand.

"Don't ever tell Daniel or Jarold I said this, but Charles is my favorite child. He's precious and special. Whenever I think of someone trying to harm him—any of my children really, but especially him—I picture myself turning into a mother tiger and lashing out. I would do anything to protect him."

"Why would you think of anyone trying to harm him?" asked Lily. "Just out of the blue?"

She woke up feeling guilty and frightened and angry at Lily.

She dimly tried to sort it out. Whey should she feel any of these things? The doctors hadn't tried to tie her tubes. There had been no conversation with Lily. She went back to sleep.

When Daniel was sixteen, he had another girlfriend. She was another small girl, with dark hair and light-brown glasses. She wrote poetry and talked a lot about feminism. Virginia still had a snapshot of them on their way to the junior prom. The girl looked embarrassed and distressed in her gown and corsage. Daniel was indifferently handsome.

Charles became a delicate, pretty adolescent. His eyes were large and green and long-lashed, his neck slender. He slouched like an arrogant little cat. Girls got crushes on him, they called and asked to speak to him in scared, high-pitched voices. He was rude to them and hung up. The only girl he liked was a homely, jittery kid who wore a leather jacket and bleached her hair. But that ended when the girl was sent to some kind of institution.

Camille got married a month after she graduated. She and Kevin flew to New Jersey for the wedding. They posed for snapshots in the den. They were radiant against the jumbled background of random shoes and scattered newspapers.

Everybody walked around the house talking and laughing and eating hunks of white cake. Kevin's father shook hands with Jarold. Kevin's mother helped in the kitchen.

Camille and Kevin went to Spain for their honeymoon. Then they moved to New York and got jobs. Camille wrote letters on heavy gray stationery with "Dr. and Mrs. Kevin Spaulding" printed across the top.

Magdalen was married the following spring. She married a Southern lawyer whom she had waited on in the health-food restaurant.

"Wouldn't you know it?" said Anne. "She probably did it to shock you. She couldn't have Camille getting all the attention."

"It's what she wanted all along," said Betty. "A daddy."

John was ten years older than Magdalen. He was broad-shouldered and slow-moving, with lazy gray eyes. Magdalen cuddled against him, her hand quiet on his lapel.

Jarold watched them with deep approval. It relaxed him to talk about them or look at them.

Virginia was happy that Magdalen had found someone normal to take care of her. She was proud of her daughter's wedding beauty and of her successful husband. She enjoyed a smug feeling of vindication now that Magdalen had come to such a conventional end.

The couple moved to John's farm in North Carolina. Magdalen baked bread and kept house. She had a baby, a fat boy named Griffin. Virginia took snapshots of Magdalen holding Griffin in a ball of blankets, her eyes startled and glistening wildly above her grin. John stood over her, his chin held high, smiling his slow-eyed smile. Magdalen asked her for advice in a meek, thrilled voice.

Virginia called Anne. "I love it," she said. "He doesn't let her get away with anything. If she gets high-toned, he puts her right in her place. And she *loves* it."

Daniel graduated from high school and then went to college to study engineering. He went with heavy sweaters, socks and boxes of records. Virginia took a picture of him standing at the train station in a huge cream-colored sweater. His tennis-shoed feet were tight together, his shoulders were hunched. He smiled tolerantly into space as a long strand of blond hair blew across his forehead and licked the lashes of one eye.

Virginia stood in the kitchen and did the dishes in the afternoon. She wore a sweatshirt and loose slacks and fat gray socks. Her hair was in a high, wispy ponytail. The sun was warm and her hands were warm in the lightly food-flecked water. The radio was on, playing love songs, songs about babies and homes. Virginia sang as she washed, about roses and bluebirds and tears of joy. She knew they were stupid songs, but they made her feel exalted. They were notations for things too important and mysterious to describe accurately in radio songs.

• • •

They had barbecues in the evenings. They ate steak and potatoes and oily salad with flowery leaves. They ate regally in their lawn chairs, looking out into their big back yard and all the trees. Charles and Jarold argued about what Charles should do after high school, or whether New York was ugly or not. Charles usually said, "Oh, never mind," and kept eating. When he was finished, he got up to walk to the stream that ran in the wooded area behind their house. Virginia and Jarold sat alone, full and splendid, their jackets around their shoulders.

Virginia loaded the dishwasher in the dimly lit kitchen, scraping the bones and greasy napkins into big black garbage bags. There was TV noise from the den, and the low rasping sound that Jarold made when he moved the newspaper. Charles came in, his face distant, his light jacket flapping. She circled his head with her arm, brought it to her shoulder and held it there to kiss before he broke from her and went away down the hall.

She sometimes sat on the couch with a pile of vinyl photo albums. One album opened on her lap to show a glanceful of red snowsuits, Christmas trees, armloads of grinning dolls, and beautiful tall children who smiled, drew pictures and were happy. Holding Easter baskets full of grass and chocolate. Raking the leaves. Winning trophies. The weddings and the graduations. The long-ribboned corsages.

She had to remind herself that Anne and Betty had families that were nice in other ways, that one of Betty's daughters was a certified genius and went to a school for advanced children.

She wrote to Anne and told her, "We're getting fat and sassy."

It was winter when Camille called. She asked how Virginia was doing and waited while Virginia told her. She asked about Magdalen and the boys. Then she said, "Mother, I'm having an abortion."

Virginia stifled a choking noise. "Were you raped?" she managed to ask.

Camille began to cry. "No," she said.

Virginia waited as Camille controlled her voice.

"No," said Camille. "Kevin doesn't want to have children. I let myself get pregnant without telling him. I thought he would change his mind, but he didn't. He's really mad. He says if I don't have an abortion, he'll divorce me."

Virginia left the phone feeling very unlike herself. She made a cup of tea and went into the den with it. She sat on the couch with one gray-socked foot propped up on the coffee table. She wondered why Kevin didn't want to have children.

She did not tell Jarold about the abortion.

Camille came home to visit. She walked around the house in her old snakeskin jumpsuit, her little hips twitching briskly. She told stories about being a corporate lawyer and teased "Daddy." Virginia admired her. But she noticed the stiff grinning lines around her mouth.

Camille visited Magdalen too. She stayed with her for two days before flying back to New York. She wrote Virginia a letter shortly afterward and told her that she felt something strange was happening between John and Magdalen. Magdalen was brittle, she said. John ordered her around a lot, in a very nasty way. She said that late one night she woke up and heard the sound of someone being rhythmically and repeatedly slapped. It went on for about five minutes. Magdalen looked fine the next day, and Camille had been too embarrassed to say anything.

Virginia called Magdalen late that night, when Jarold was in bed. She didn't hear anything strange in her voice. When Virginia got off the phone, she put on an old gray sweater and walked from room to room. The rooms were dark and hollow. They seemed unfamiliar and eerie, but that didn't make her go upstairs or turn on the light. She stood in the middle of the dark living room with her feet together, wrapping the sweater around her. She stood there not thinking about anything, just hearing the wind and the faint hum of the house.

Charles and Jarold had a fight. Charles was graduating from high school and he didn't want to go to college. He just wanted to move out of the house. Jarold told him his attitude was stupid and weak. "Magdalen thought she'd go the unconventional, freaky route," said Jarold at breakfast, "and look where it got her. Married, a mother. And happy for the first time in her mixed-up life."

"I still think Magdalen's freaky," said Charles.

It went on for about a week. Then Charles lost his temper. He said, "I'd rather be on my face in the Bowery than be a horse's ass like you."

"Charles," said Virginia.

Jarold crossed the room and belted Charles across the face, knocking him out of his chair. Virginia dropped her glass in the sink and ran to Charles. "Don't you dare hit my son!" she screamed.

"Oh, get out of here, you idiot," said Charles. He wiped the blood from his mouth in a bored way.

Virginia began sitting up late at night in the den, drinking and staring at her gray feet. She made sarcastic comments that nobody paid any attention to. Jarold called her "Mother." "Now, Mother," he'd say.

Charles moved to New York. He got a job in a record store and an apartment on the Lower East Side of Manhattan. Other than that, it was hard to tell what he was doing.

Virginia called Camille. Camille was meeting wonderful new people and being successful. She told lots of funny stories. But then she said, "I don't know if I should tell you this, but I'm having a hard time keeping it to myself. Last month Magdalen told me that John slapped her. Not hard or anything. But still."

She paused so Virginia could say something. Virginia sat quietly and stared at the kitchen.

"Of course, we both know how annoying Magdalen can be," continued Camille. "But that doesn't give him the right to strike her."

Virginia left the conversation feeling cheated. Camille had told her about Magdalen at the end of the conversation, after all the good things. That seemed strange to Virginia. She sat for a long time on the stool under the phone with her legs tightly crossed and her elbows on the knee of one leg. She thought about how awful the kitchen was. There were balls of dust and tiny crumbs around the edges of the floor. Pans full of greasy water ranged across the counter. The top of the refrigerator was black. Everything in the room seemed disconnected from its purpose.

In the fall, Daniel decided that he didn't like engineering school and dropped out. Jarold argued with him over the phone for a long time. When he hung up, Jarold went out into the garage and sat in the car with a scarf around his neck. He sat there for over an hour. Virginia could hear the car's engine start, chug awkwardly, and then shut off. This happened several times. She couldn't tell whether Jarold was repeatedly deciding to drive somewhere and then changing his mind, or if he was just keeping warm.

Camille divorced Kevin two months later. She put her things in bags and boxes and moved into a girlfriend's apartment. She tried to make it sound like fun. Virginia pictured her sitting on the couch with her friend, both of them bundled in blankets, drinking mugs of tea, being supportive. It was a nice picture, but it seemed adolescent.

Everybody came home for the holidays. Magdalen and Camille hugged each other constantly during the visit. On Christmas they wore their pajamas and slippers all day. They sat close together and squeezed each other's hands. They had confidential conversations, which Virginia only half heard. When the talked to anyone else, their faces stiffened slightly. Magdalen had a hard time finishing a sentence.

No one else seemed to notice. "Magdalen's always been flighty," said Jarold.

Charles was very pale. He picked at the Christmas meal, eating very little. His dinner plate was a mass of picked-apart food. Daniel ate a lot. He ate while he talked or walked through the room. There were often light brown crumbs on his plaid shirt.

Virginia took only one group picture. It came out ugly. Magdalen's eyes were a dazed green slur. Camille's neck was rigid and stretched, her eyes bulged. Daniel's eyes were rolled up and his nostrils were flared. Charles hung back on the couch, his hand covering the face of a malignant elf. Jarold, half in the picture and seen from the side, was frozen in the middle of a senseless gesture.

Virginia and Jarold were in the den watching the late movie when Magdalen called. Virginia tried to ignore the phone. It rang eight times. "Are you going to get that, honey?" said Jarold.

Magdalen's voice was calm. "Mama, I'm calling from the bus station in Charleston. John and I had a fight. He broke my nose. Griffin and I are coming home."

She arrived at 4:30 in the morning. Virginia stood at the door in a flannel nightgown watching the taxi pull into the driveway. Magdalen emerged in the open-car-door light, a thin girl in a bulky army coat. The door shut and she became a slow, bundled figure kicking the driveway gravel with her shuffling steps. "Mom?" Her voice was sheepish and sweet.

She carried one suitcase and a big shopping bag. Griffin had just started walking. He looked tired and wistful. His blond hair was much too long.

John called the house, but they hung up on him. He threatened to come and get Magdalen, but Jarold said he'd kill him if he did.

Magdalen found a small apartment in town. She got a job at a flower shop. Virginia took care of Griffin during the day while Magdalen was at work. Griffin was a shy, pensive child who talked in bursts. He was precise, analytical and watchful. He made Virginia feel protective and sad. She tried hard to keep her sadness from showing.

After a few months the florist let Magdalen take the flowers home so she could be with Griffin.

On weekends Magdalen and Virginia went shopping for clothes or groceries. They were quiet and easy with each other. Magdalen lent Virginia books to read, and they talked about them.

Virginia was surprised at how nice it was to be in Magdalen's apartment. She liked to go there in the mornings with cherry-cheese pastry or fruit. Magdalen would be in the large, bare main room, sitting in her cotton robe on a floor pillow. The sun would come in through a big, curtainless window. There were white plastic buckets of roses, tulips, irises, freesia, dyed carnations, birds of paradise and wild magenta daisies. There were bunches of flowers on the floor on wet, unrolled newspaper. Stripped rose thorns lay on the paper like lost baby teeth.

Magdalen's movements were nimble and quick. Her face was serene and beautiful. She seemed completely content.

Virginia felt as though she were a total stranger.

Virginia and Jarold became very quiet together. They still watched late-night movies, but they rarely sat cuddled together. Jarold got tired early and went upstairs to bed. He was always asleep when Virginia came up.

Sometimes she thought Jarold looked obtuse and stupid. At breakfast, when he bent over the paper, he frowned so hard that his mouth pulled his entire face downward and he looked like a shark. His eyes were disapproving. His nose became blunt as a snout.

She knew that he thought his children were failures.

Camille found a wonderful apartment. She began dating a man whom she liked a lot. She came to New Jersey often. She usually stayed with Magdalen. Virginia would take them all for a drive in the mountains. They ate ice cream and made family jokes. The girls would lie all over the back seat and giggle, Camille's hand on Magdalen's thigh, one tilting her head against the other's shoulder.

It was early morning when they found out about Charles. Jarold had just gotten into the shower. The clock radio, wavering between two stations, interlaced the weather report with a song about dumping your girlfriend. Virginia felt her forehead wrinkling as she tried to ignore the noise. She burrowed her head into the pillow and listened to the warm, dull whish of the shower. The phone rang. She opened her eyes; the red digits said 6:15. She wouldn't have answered if it hadn't kept ringing so long.

• • •

He had been driving from upstate New York in a friend's car. He had been drinking. He'd passed a truck coming around a turn, collided with another car and gone off the road. His car flipped over and caught fire. His car was badly burned. The other driver survived.

Virginia's life became a set of events with no meaning or relationship to one another. She was a cold planet orbiting for no reason in a galaxy of remote, silent movement. The house was a series of objects that she had to avoid bumping into. Food would not go down her throat. The faces of her husband and children were abstract patterns taking on various shapes to symbolize various messages. It was exhausting to keep track of them.

She slept on the couch in the den every night. At first it just happened that way. She'd be sitting before the TV with her glass of Scotch when Jarold would kiss the top of her head and go upstairs. She'd go into the kitchen and get a bottle and drink from it. She'd watch the chartreuse-and-violet people walk around the screen. It was sometimes a comfort.

She fell asleep on the hard little throw pillow. She always woke up with sweat around her collar and a stiff neck.

One night Jarold took her hand and said, "Come on, honey. Come to bed. You'll fall asleep on the couch if you don't."

"I want to fall asleep on the couch," said Virginia.

"No, you don't," said Jarold. He tugged her arm. "It's unhealthy. Come into your nice warm bed."

She yanked her hand out of his. "I don't want to sleep in the bed."

It was true. She couldn't bear the thought of lying next to him. He could see it in her eyes and it wounded him. He walked away. He said nothing about it again.

Magdalen came to see her almost every day. She walked around the kitchen cleaning things while Virginia sat at the table. Virginia watched her long, calm hands closing cabinets, sorting silverware, rubbing surfaces with wet, stained old cloths. She remembered how Magdalen used to run around and make so much noise. It was a clear memory, but it didn't seem as though it was hers.

Virginia began getting up to cook Jarold's breakfast again. She put an extra alarm clock beside the couch. She put on a robe over her rumpled clothes and moved around the kitchen. She put her plate of eggs opposite Jarold's and ate them. Jarold's jaws chewed stiffly; his throat was like wood. But they talked, and she found it comforting.

Before he left he would hold her hand and kiss her. She'd wait until he was gone, then sit back down again and cry.

Charles had been dead eight months when Anne came.

Virginia drove to the airport to pick her up. It was strange to be at the wheel of a car again, driving with a lot of other cars around her. It was very sunny, and the primary-colored metal of the cars was festive in the brightness. She turned the radio on and rolled down the window.

Anne was waiting at the terminal in a gray suit. When she saw Virginia she tipped her head to the side and grinned; she raised her hand and waved it in stiff, frantic waves.

They hugged. Anne only came up to Virginia's chest. Still hugging, they leaned back to look at each other and laughed. Anne's glasses were cockeyed. "Goodness, you've gotten thin," she said. "Let's take you home and feed you. I'm starved."

They rode through traffic, chattering. Virginia didn't go straight home. She left the highway and drove up into the mountains. Anne rolled down her window and put her gray elbow on the ledge. She said, "It's simply glorious up here."

They had egg sandwiches and fruit for lunch. Virginia had cleaned the kitchen and put a vase of pink and white carnations on the table. The fruit was cut up in a large cream-colored bowl. They helped themselves at a leisurely pace, sometimes eating the wet, lightly bruised fruit straight from the bowl with their fingers. The afternoon sun came in, lighting up a sparkling flurry of dust flecks.

• • •

Virginia talked about Camille, Daniel and Magdalen. She told Anne about Camille's career success and about how helpful Magdalen was. "She still lives like a hippie, though. I don't think she misses the big ranch they had at all. She certainly doesn't miss John. The only time she's ever mentioned him was to say that she was always surprised at how stupid he turned out to be. It's weird. It's like it never happened."

"Well, you know some people work best in that kind of foot-loose life-style," said Anne. "It's called being a bohemian. Lily's still that way."

"Is she doing well?"

"Oh, yes. You know, I don't ever worry about her anymore. Ever since she's gotten serious about photography, her whole life's pulled together. She really works hard. She works for all the papers and magazines in Detroit."

Virginia looked at the pieces of fruit on her plate. "I always thought that Lily could do well if she wanted to," she said. "She was such a sensitive child. I was sorry I couldn't do anything to help her."

"Don't feel that way. You couldn't have done anything. She was too difficult."

"Yes," said Virginia. "She was."

"But she has good memories of you," said Anne. "She used to tell me about going up into the mountains with you. She said that the two of you ate so many olives in the living room together that for years the color of olives made her think of you." Anne grinned in a hideously open way.

Virginia looked at the fruit.

"And then do you know what she said? She said, 'But that's not right because Virginia's not like an olive color at all. She's more golden.'"

"Oh, stop it," said Virginia.

"But that's how I always thought of you too, even when you were awful. You were always golden."

Anne was smiling again, her eyes in sad half-moons. She saw

that Virginia was embarrassed, so she looked down and picked up a wet piece of melon. She ate it, smiling dimly. The movements of her jaw were neat and careful.

Virginia was afraid for a moment that she was going to say something nasty to Anne, though she wasn't sure why. She had a drink of coffee instead. It was getting cold and oily.

"What's wrong?" Anne was watching her with a dark, naked look.

Virginia glanced away. "Nothing."

They had an old-fashioned family barbecue for Anne's visit. It was the first one they'd had in a year, and Jarold was excited about it. He was ceremonious and manly beside the smoking barbecue, pronged fork in hand. Anne nervously mixed the salad and talked to Jarold about her job counseling old people in Detroit. Magdalen came out of the house, bringing a flat dish of cold pasta. She put the dish on the card table and her hand on Virginia's shoulder. "How are you doing, Mama? Did you and Anne have a good time?"

"We had a lovely time. We went for a long drive in the mountains."

"Oh, yes," said Anne. "We actually got out of the car and *walked* for a long time. I was enthralled. It was just gorgeous."

"Anne must've put a pound of rocks in her pockets," said Virginia. "Every time I turned around, she was picking up something else."

"I love it up there," said Magdalen. "It's my salvation." She moved lightly around the card table, folding napkins.

"You know, something I've noticed since I've gotten older is my sensitivity to nature," said Anne. "When I was very young—a teenager—the sight of a sunset or a mountain scene was so deeply moving to me, I would get the chills." She looked at Magdalen and shivered her shoulders. "And then, as I entered my twenties, I lost that sensitivity."

"Well, I'm sure it wasn't lost. You just had to concentrate on other things," said Virginia.

"I suppose," said Anne. "But there came a point when I hardly responded to nature at all. I still liked it, but it didn't move me. Now that I'm on the verge of becoming an old lady, I'm starting to respond to nature again, to be stirred by the great outdoors." She looked at Jarold with vulnerable eyes, her glasses down on her nose.

"That's wonderful," he said. "It shows you're still excited by life. And that's the most important thing to keep through the years, more important than money or success. A lot of us lose it."

"I believe that," said Anne. "That's why I enjoy working with old folks. It's marvelous to watch some of them blossom again, especially the ones who've been in those horrible nursing homes. They can be like kids with the openness—it's exciting to give them another chance to experience it."

"You're a very giving person," said Jarold. He looked at Anne with tender, protective awe, a little shamed, as if he knew that giving was beyond his ability but he was glad that somebody was there to do it.

It was strange to Virginia. When they were young, Jarold thought Anne was silly and too serious and a frump besides. Now here he was, thirty years later, looking at her like that.

"The steaks are ready," said Jarold.

Magdalen put the steaks on the plates. Anne and Virginia arranged servings of salad and pasta. They all sat in lawn chairs and ate from the warm plates in their laps. The steak was good and rare; its juices ran into the salad and pasta when Virginia moved her knees. A light wind blew loose hairs around their faces and tickled them. The trees rustled dimly. There were nice insect noises.

Jarold paused, a forkful of steak rising across his chest. "Like heaven," he said. "It's like heaven."

They were quiet for several minutes.

About the Author

MARY GAITSKILL is the author of *Don't Cry; Veronica,* a National Book Award finalist; *Because They Wanted To,* which was nominated for a PEN/Faulkner Award; and *Two Girls, Fat and Thin.* A recipient of a Guggenheim Fellowship for fiction, her work has appeared in *The New Yorker, Harper's, Esquire, The Best American Short Stories,* and *The O. Henry Prize Stories.*